She'd Fo...

She just stared at R... seen him before in her life. She'd been viewing him not as her buddy, but as the father of her child. The whole concept was so strange, new and foreign that she'd failed to inhale, then exhale.

But she was fine now. She was in control. Richard was the same old Richard. Granted, he looked like a million dollars.

"Hey, want to hear some trivia from Detroit?" he said. "Brenda, did you know that a shark is the only fish that can blink with both eyes…? So what have you got for me? Lay some new trivia on your buddy here."

"Richard, I'm…I'm pregnant…with your baby."

Dear Reader,

Thanks to all who have shared, in letters and at our Web site, eHarlequin.com, how much you love Silhouette Desire! One Web visitor told us, "When I was nineteen, this man broke my heart. So I picked up a Silhouette Desire and...lost myself in other people's happiness, sorrow, desire.... Guys came and went and the books kept entertaining me." It is so gratifying to know how our books have touched and even changed your lives—especially with Silhouette celebrating our 20th anniversary in 2000.

The incomparable Joan Hohl dreamed up October's MAN OF THE MONTH. *The Dakota Man* is used to getting his way until he meets his match in a feisty jilted bride. And Anne Marie Winston offers you a *Rancher's Proposition,* which is part of the highly sensual Desire promotion BODY & SOUL.

First Comes Love is another sexy love story by Elizabeth Bevarly. A virgin finds an unexpected champion when she is rumored to be pregnant. The latest installment of the sensational Desire miniseries FORTUNE'S CHILDREN: THE GROOMS is *Fortune's Secret Child* by Shawna Delacorte. Maureen Child's popular BACHELOR BATTALION continues with *Marooned with a Marine.* And Joan Elliott Pickart returns to Desire with *Baby: MacAllister-Made,* part of her wonderful miniseries THE BABY BET.

So take your own emotional journey through our six new powerful, passionate, provocative love stories from Silhouette Desire—and keep sending us those letters and e-mails, sharing your enthusiasm for our books!

Enjoy!

Joan Marlow Golan

Joan Marlow Golan
Senior Editor, Silhouette Desire

Please address questions and book requests to:
Silhouette Reader Service
U.S.: 3010 Walden Ave., P.O. Box 1325, Buffalo, NY 14269
Canadian: P.O. Box 609, Fort Erie, Ont. L2A 5X3

Baby:
MacAllister-Made
JOAN ELLIOTT PICKART

Silhouette®
Desire
Published by Silhouette Books
America's Publisher of Contemporary Romance

For Scooter
Give lots of hugs to Cricket, Scoo

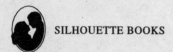

SILHOUETTE BOOKS

ISBN 0-373-76326-3

BABY: MACALLISTER-MADE

Copyright © 2000 by Joan Elliott Pickart

Visit Silhouette at www.eHarlequin.com

Printed in U.S.A.

JOAN ELLIOTT PICKART

is the author of over eighty novels. When she isn't writing, she enjoys watching football, knitting, reading, gardening and attending craft shows on the town square. Joan has three all-grown-up daughters and a fantastic little grandson. In September of 1995 Joan traveled to China to adopt her fourth daughter, Autumn. Joan and Autumn have settled into their cozy cottage in a charming small town in the high pine country of Arizona.

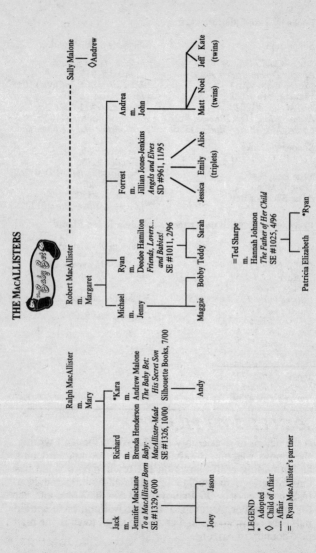

THE MacALLISTERS

The Baby Bet

Ralph MacAllister
m.
Mary

Robert MacAllister
m.
Margaret

Sally Malone

◇Andrew

Ralph MacAllister line:

Jack   Richard   *Kara   Andrew Malone
m.   m.   *The Baby Bet:*
Jennifer Mackane   Brenda Henderson   *His Secret Son*
To a MacAllister Born *MacAllister-Made*   Silhouette Books, 7/00
SE #1329, 6/00   *Baby:*
                    SE #1326, 10/00

Joey   Jason   Andy

Robert MacAllister line:

Michael   Ryan   Forrest   Andrea
m.   m.   m.   m.
Jenny   Dedee Hamilton Jillian Jones-Jenkins John
                    Friends, Lovers... *Angels and Elves*
                    and Babies!   SD #961, 11/95
                    SE #1011, 2/96

Maggie Bobby Teddy Sarah   Jessica Emily Alice   Matt Noel Jeff Kate
                                 (triplets)   (twins)   (twins)

=Ted Sharpe
m.
Hannah Johnson
The Father of Her Child
SE #1025, 4/96

Patricia Elizabeth   *Ryan

LEGEND
* Adopted
◇ Child of Affair
---- Affair
= Ryan MacAllister's partner

One

Richard MacAllister entered his apartment and slammed the door closed behind him. He shrugged out of his sport coat, tossed it onto a chair, then picked it up in the next instant and strode into his bedroom to hang it in the closet in its proper color-coordinated place.

He returned to the living room and slouched onto the sofa, then rose again to pace restlessly around the large room.

"Women," he muttered. "Who needs them? They're all fickle. Weird. Totally unreliable, unpredictable, ununderstandable...except that's probably not a word. Oh, man, women drive me nuts."

Richard halted his trek, shoved both hands through his hair, then strode to the far wall of the living room and pounded on it loudly with three solid thumps.

"Be home," he said, staring at the wall. "At a time like this a person needs to talk to his best friend. Come on, come on, let me know that you're there."

Two muffled knocks sounded through the wall, which Richard returned quickly with one thunk.

Good, he thought. Message sent, received and answered. Three knocks to determine if anyone was home, two knocks acknowledging that fact, then one to communicate the directive to please come over. Primitive, yes, but it worked. And, besides, it was fun, a secret code known only to him and his buddy.

In a few moments his best friend would arrive to listen to his current tale of woe, provide a shoulder, react with the appropriate sympathy and comforting pat on the back that was called for.

Granted, Richard thought, he was a grown man, who was perfectly capable of dealing with his own emotions, licking his own wounds, pulling himself up by the bootstraps and carrying on. Yes, of course he was. But why suffer alone when he knew that his best buddy was willing to share his misery?

A knock on the apartment door was music to Richard's ears, and he hurried to fling open the door, speaking at the same time.

"I'm so glad to see you," he said. "I really am bummed and... Uh-oh. This is *not* good. You're wearing your pea-soup robe, which means you must feel *very* lousy to have dragged that disaster out of the closet. What's wrong with you, Brenda?"

Richard narrowed his eyes and scrutinized the woman who was standing before him.

Brenda was definitely not her usual chipper self, he thought. Her slender figure was covered from neck to toe in the awful, faded chenille robe the color of pea soup, a sure sign that she wasn't up to par. That robe was her comfort blankie, used only when she was physically ill or emotionally bottomed out.

From the roll of paper towels tucked under one arm and the way she was dabbing at her red-tipped nose, he surmised that Brenda was physically ill. As well, her pretty, delicate features were pale, and her brown eyes, which usually sparkled, were sort of blurry.

"May I come in, Richard?" Brenda said, then sighed and patted her nose with the paper towel again.

"What? Oh, sure. I'm sorry," he said, stepping back to allow her room to enter. "I was just checking you over. You look like hell, Bren."

Brenda glared at him as she shuffled past him, her feet encased in oversize athletic socks that actually belonged to Richard.

"Thanks a lot," she said, flopping onto the sofa. "That's just what I needed to hear. You're so great for a woman's morale."

Richard perched on the coffee table in front of Brenda, and she slid her gaze over him, just as he had done to her, wrinkling her nose in the process.

"You don't get any awards for appearance, either, Richard," she said. "Your hair is sticking out, which means you've been dragging your hands through it. You have dark circles under your eyes. Your tan went south while you were in Kansas City, too."

"Yeah, well…"

"You're still handsome as all get-out," Brenda rambled, "but your hair needs a trim. That's the hair that one of your sweetie-pies of yesteryear told me was yummy. Thick and yummy. Oh, please, give me a break. Yummy?

"Granted, it's nice hair, light brown and sun-streaked in places, but at the moment, as I pointed out, it looks like you stuck your finger in an electrical socket. On a scale of one to ten, you're a five."

Richard smoothed his hair into place with both hands, then leaned close to Brenda.

"Are you sick?" he said, frowning. "That you're in a lousy, crabby mood is obvious, but do you have a dread disease?"

"Yep. I'm going to be dead by midnight. Good-bye, Richard. I just want you to know that you've been a wonderful best friend for the past fourteen months, and I—"

"Would you cut it out?" he said. "What disease do you have?"

"A roaring sinus infection," Brenda said, then sighed as she dabbed at her nose. "I felt so terrible yesterday that I actually went to the doctor and he gave me an antibiotic to take. But plucky little thing that I am, I went out on my blind date last night, anyway."

"I thought you swore you'd never again go on a blind date."

"I was desperate," she said, sighing again. "This guy was the friend of the cousin of one of the clients of the travel agency. A dentist. He's a dentist. He spent the entire evening staring at my teeth."

Richard laughed, then sobered in the next instant as Brenda glowered at him.

"I kid you not, Richard," she said. "Every time

I smiled he just zeroed in on my front teeth. He spoke to my teeth, you know what I mean? When he brought me home, he put his arms around me, told me I had the nicest teeth he'd seen in a very long while, then kissed me on the forehead.

"I'd dragged myself out of my sick bed to go out with that weird biscuit. Never again. No more blind dates for me. Not ever. In fact, I just might give up on men."

"Join the club," Richard said, nodding.

"Oh? You're giving up on men?" she said, then laughed.

"Cute." Richard got to his feet and placed the edge of one hand against his throat. "I've had it up to here with the female species." He paused. "Why are you using paper towels on your poor red nose?"

"I didn't have any tissues," Brenda said. "I wrote tissues on my shopping list but—"

"Yeah, I know, you lost the list. What happened to the penguin magnet I brought you from Alaska? That was supposed to hold your shopping list on your refrigerator."

"I can't find it," Brenda said. "The magnet. I don't know where the magnet is. The refrigerator is still in its designated spot, though."

"Stay put. I can't stand the punishment you're dishing out to your pert little nose."

Richard started across the room.

"Pert little nose?" Brenda yelled. "Want to meet the dentist? He flipped out over my teeth. Now if I can find some yo-yo who is bonkers for my eyes, I'll have my entire face being worshipped by wackos."

"Put a cork in it," Richard said, as he disappeared from the living room.

He returned moments later with a freshly laundered, neatly folded cotton handkerchief. He pulled the roll of paper towels from beneath Brenda's arm, set it on the coffee table, then smacked the handkerchief into her hand.

"There. Use that," he said, then slouched onto the sofa next to her.

"Thank you." Brenda dotted her nose with the hankie. "Oh, this so nice and soft. It smells like lemons, too. I'll wash it and return it to you later."

"No, you won't," Richard said, resting his head on the top of the sofa and staring at the ceiling. "You'll lose it somewhere between the washing machine and the dryer."

"That's not fair," Brenda said with an indignant sniff. "You refuse to believe me when I tell you that the washing machines in the laundry room in this building eat my stuff. They really do. Of course, you wouldn't know that because you send everything out to your fancy-dancy place and have it all professionally laundered. Big la-di-da deal."

"Whatever," Richard said. "Okay, the washing machines gobble up your stuff."

Brenda frowned and shifted on the sofa so she could get a better look at Richard.

"You're giving in on the washing machines?" she said. "Just like that? No argument? Goodness, you really are in a lower-than-low mood. What happened? Even more, *when* did whatever it is happen? I didn't even know that you were back from Kansas City."

"I flew in late this afternoon," he said, still focusing on the ceiling. "Exhausted to the bone. I'd called Beverly from Kansas City last night and made a date with her. I was really looking forward to it, to seeing her, having a great time and—ha! What a joke."

"What went wrong?"

Richard turned his head to look at Brenda. "She broke up with me, Bren. She found somebody else while I was away. The jerk is a stockbroker. Beverly said that being in a relationship with a computer troubleshooter was like being a nun in a convent, because all she did was stay in her apartment while I was out of town."

"She has a valid point there," Brenda said thoughtfully.

"Oh, thanks a bunch," he said, none too quietly. "Whose side are you on here? I just got dumped, Bren. I'd like a bit of sympathy if it isn't too much trouble on your part, buddy."

"Well, cripe, Richard, what do you want me to say? Let's take an honest look at this situation. You left for Alaska right after the new year, once you knew that your uncle Robert was going to recover from his heart attack and the surgery that followed."

"So?"

"So, you were gone for almost two months," she said, holding up the appropriate number of fingers. "You came home, met Beverly at a party and saw her nearly every night for what...three or four weeks?"

"And what dynamite weeks those were," he said, a wistful tone to his voice. "Whew."

"Spare me the details." Brenda wiped her nose with the soft handkerchief. "Then you left for Kansas City and you've been gone for a month." She paused. "What did you expect Beverly to do? You'd only been seeing each other for a few weeks and then...poof...you disappear, unable even to tell her when you'd be back in Ventura."

"I never know how long I'll be gone. You know that," Richard said. "It depends on what I discover when I get to the job site, what the problem is with the company's computer system."

"I realize that, Richard, but *I* miss you when you're gone. Imagine how someone who has romantic feelings feels. Beverly obviously cared for you, but your relationship was too new for that kind of a separation. She bailed out before she got hurt. I'm sorry, sweet friend, but I really see where she was coming from."

"You're not doing one damn thing to lift me out of my state of total depression, Brenda," Richard said, frowning at her.

"Sorry, bub, but I calls 'em as I sees 'em," Brenda said, shrugging. "Face it, Richard. You're going to have a tough, if not impossible, time finding a woman to marry and have the children you want so badly if you insist on keeping the job that you have.

"All the traveling you do is killing off your budding romances, due to the lack of appropriate nurturing.... Gracious, I'm certainly profound. when I have a sinus infection."

"I am now officially beyond depressed," Richard said, staring at the ceiling again. "Some best friend you are, Brenda Henderson. You've pushed me right over the edge of my misery into a bleak, dark void of nothingness.''

''I think that's redundant, Richard.''

''Oh. Well, you get the drift. I don't want to talk about this anymore.'' Richard got to his feet. ''We're going to celebrate.''

''What on earth do we have to celebrate?'' Brenda said, as Richard headed toward the kitchen.

''I don't have a clue,'' he said. ''We'll think of something. Got any new trivia for me?''

''I've got a beaut,'' Brenda said, sitting up straighter on the sofa.

Richard returned with a bottle of wine and two crystal glasses. He filled the glasses, handed one to Brenda, then raised his high in the air.

''Here's to us,'' he said. ''Best friends…in good times and bad…the present Saturday night we are now experiencing being just about as lousy as it gets.'' He suddenly paused. ''Whoa. Wait. I don't think you're supposed to drink alcohol while you're taking antibiotics.''

''There's a sticker on the prescription bottle that says something about that, but this isn't exactly one hundred proof whiskey. A little bit of wine shouldn't do any harm. It might even make me relax and feel better because I'm so-o-o stressed.''

''Well, okay,'' Richard said slowly, ''but I'm limiting your intake of the grape, Miss.''

They clinked their glasses, took sips of the delicious wine, then Richard sat back down next to Brenda.

"Lay some trivia on me. It'll cheer me up," he said, then drained his glass.

"This is a lovely wine," Brenda said. "These antibiotics I'm taking make me so thirsty. That went down as smoothly as velvet stroking my parched throat."

Richard refilled his glass. "Trivia, please, my dear Ms. Henderson?"

"Certainly, Mr. MacAllister. Try this on for size. Did you know that rubber bands last longer if you store them in the refrigerator?" She raised her eyebrows. "How's that?"

"Not bad," Richard said, nodding in approval. "Not bad at all. Remind me to put my rubber bands in the fridge. No, forget it. You'll write yourself a note to remind yourself to remind me, then you'll lose the note."

"Yep." Brenda laughed, then emptied her glass in three swallows. "Very, very smooth wine. It's warming me right down to my toes." She raised her feet and wiggled them, causing the oversize socks to slip off and land in a heap on the floor. "Did you bring some trivia from Kansas City?"

"Indeed I did, my poor sick pal," he said.

Richard picked up the socks, folded them neatly, set them on the coffee table, then slid one arm across Brenda's shoulders. She nestled close to him, patting her nose as she settled into a more comfortable position.

"Ready for trivia, compliments of Kansas City?" Richard said.

"I certainly am," Brenda said, nodding, "but would you fill my glass first, please?"

"Nope. You can have one inch more and that's it. Let's not push our luck with the mixing of wine and antibiotics, Bren. It worries me."

"One more inch is fine," she said. "I'm mellowing out already as it is."

Richard poured a carefully measured amount of wine into Brenda's glass, then moved back again.

"Okay," he said. "Here comes the trivia. May I have a drum roll, please, ma'am? This is much better than your frozen rubber bands."

"Forget the drum."

"Right. Ms. Henderson, I hereby inform you that there are 293 ways to make change for a dollar."

Richard emptied his glass, placed it on the coffee table, then turned his head and dropped a quick kiss on Brenda's nose.

"How about that trivia, kid?" he said. "Kind of knocks you out, doesn't it? Leaves you speechless?" He paused. "Cancel that part. *Nothing* would leave you speechless. You'll still be expressing your opinion about something when you knock on the pearly gates."

"You're probably right about that." Brenda laughed, then hiccuped.

"So? How did you like the dollar bill trivia?"

"Super," she said, nodding. "Definitely beats my keeping rubber bands in the veggie crisper." She leaned forward and kissed Richard on the cheek. "You win this round, no doubt about it."

"Good for me," Richard said, then stifled a yawn. "Man, I'm beat. I put in sixteen- and eighteen-hour days in Kansas, then came home and got the shaft from Betty. Life really stinks at times."

"Richard, her name was Beverly. Beverly, not Betty."

"Oh, yeah…Beverly," he said, then frowned. "Oh, well, easy come, easy go. Do I believe that? No. Do I believe that sometimes life really stinks? Yes."

"Hey, don't be gloomy," Brenda said. "You just won high marks for your trivia. That's very important, you know. Yep, that's a biggy."

"What's my prize?" he said, looking at her again.

"You get to kiss the loser," she said, then puckered her lips in an exaggerated fashion and closed her eyes.

Richard planted a loud, smacking kiss on Brenda's lips, then hesitated a fraction of a second and kissed her again, gently this time, so very softly.

Brenda's lips seemed to melt under Richard's, parting slightly to allow his questing tongue to delve into her mouth to meet her tongue. She returned the sensual demands of his lips and tongue in total abandon.

Brenda? Hello? she thought hazily. What were they doing? She and Richard MacAllister were kissing?

Well, sure, they gave each other little pecks all the time and—but, oh, dear heaven, this was no best-buddy peck. This was a man kissing a woman, the real goods.

They shouldn't be doing this. Nope. No way. And she was going to end this kiss right now. Well, soon. Later. Next week.

A soft purr of feminine pleasure escaped from Brenda's throat as the kiss went on and on.

MacAllister! Get a grip, Richard admonished himself. He didn't kiss Brenda like this. Not like *this*. But, oh, man, she was responding to him totally, sending him up in flames. Her lips were so soft, so responsive, so— No, this was wrong. This was Brenda, his buddy, his best friend. This was crazy. This was...sensational.

A masculine groan rumbled in Richard's chest. He wrapped his arms around Brenda as her hands encircled his neck, their lips meeting once more. He slid down onto the plush cushions of the sofa without breaking the kiss, taking Brenda with him, then shifted them both until she was stretched out on top of him.

The sash of Brenda's robe had loosened a bit during the motions, and the material slid off one of her shoulders.

Richard blinked, then blinked again as he saw her bare, dewy skin close to his somewhat unfocused eyes. He tightened his hold on Brenda, then rolled them over to place her beneath him, nearly toppling them off the sofa. He supported his weight on one forearm, then trailed nibbling kisses across her bare shoulder, then lower to where the material stopped just above her breast.

"What..." Richard said, his voice gritty. "What do you have on underneath that thing?"

"Hmm?" Brenda said dreamily. "Oh. I don't have anything on. Nothing. I'd just gotten out of a long, warm, bubble bath when you knocked on the wall. I didn't take the time to dress before I came over, just put on my old, comfy robe. I put the pea-soup over my birthday suit. How's that for trivia?"

"That's not exactly trivia," Richard said, shaking his head slightly. "Not even close. I'm going to kiss you again now, Brenda, because I really need to do that."

Richard lowered his head and kissed Brenda with such intensity that she felt as though he was stealing the very breath from her body. She was suffused with heat, and a pulsing began low within her, making it impossible to think, rendering her capable of only feeling, savoring...wanting.

Wanting Richard.

Burning with desire for Richard MacAllister.

Nagging voices of disapproval sounded in Richard's brain and he ignored them, allowed passion to consume his mind and aroused body.

He was on fire.

Nothing mattered but the intensity of his want and need for Brenda, which was far beyond anything he had ever experienced before. And she wanted him. *Him.* She felt so damn good, and tasted like fine wine, and smelled like flowers from the bubble bath she'd taken.

She'd been naked in that bath, the zillions of bubbles dancing over her soft skin, clinging here, there, everywhere and...

Richard untied the sash, then brushed away the heavy material of the robe, exposing the half of Brenda's body that wasn't covered with his own body.

Bubbles here, he thought foggily, lowering his mouth to her breast, then laving the nipple to a taut bud with his tongue.

"Mmm," Brenda said.

Richard traveled lower.

And bubbles here, he mentally rambled, kissing the dewy skin on Brenda's flat stomach. Lucky little bubbles, those bubbles.

He returned to her breast, drawing the sweet bounty deep into his mouth. Brenda sank her fingers into his thick hair, urging his mouth more firmly onto her breast, her breath catching.

Richard's sun-streaked light brown hair really *was* yummy, Brenda thought, from a faraway place in her misty mind. So thick and silky. Lovely hair. Just divine.

Oh, she felt so strange. But wonderful. She'd never experienced such all-consuming passion, such driving need, such burning want. She couldn't bear this anymore. She had to quell this fire before there was nothing left of her except cinders that would be blown away by the wind.

"Richard, please," she whispered, her voice holding the echo of a sob. "I want you so much. Please."

"I want you, too, Brenda," he said, not recognizing the sound of his own voice. "But…"

"Don't think. We don't have to think, do we, Richard? Tell me we don't have to think."

"We don't have to think," he said thickly. "No thinking. None. Oh, hell…wait. Birth control. Better think about that one."

"I'm on the Pill," she said. "No problem."

"That ends the thinking," he said.

"Oh, thank goodness."

Richard leveled himself to his feet and shed his clothes quickly, flinging them onto the floor. Brenda visually traced every magnificent inch of him as though she'd never seen him before, despite the fact that they'd both been clad in bathing suits on several occasions in the past, when she'd attended MacAllister gatherings with him.

But this was very different, Brenda's mind hummed. This was now. This wasn't Richard her buddy, her best friend, her pal. Before her stood Richard the man and, oh, mercy, he was so blatantly *male* that it defied description.

It was as though she was suddenly wearing a pair of magical glasses that were causing her to view him as she never had before. Incredible.

Richard reached down and scooped Brenda into his arms, lifting her to his chest and leaving the pea-soup robe behind.

He kissed her deeply, and she returned the kiss in kind as she entwined her arms around his neck. He broke the kiss and strode across the room, down the hall and into his bedroom. He set her on her feet next to the bed, swept back the blankets, then placed her in the center of the big bed, following her down to lie next to her.

So beautiful, Richard thought, as his mouth captured Brenda's once again. Brenda was exquisite, so delicate and feminine, making him so acutely aware of his own size and masculinity.

He'd always considered her to be pretty in a fresh, wholesome way, but right now, at this moment in time, Brenda was the most sensuous, enticing, tantalizing woman he had ever seen in his entire life.

He'd known since he met her on that fateful day when they'd both moved into their new apartments at the same time that Brenda was funny, thoughtful and caring. They'd discovered very early on that they were poles apart on so many issues that they never could be more than friends, so friends they were…best friends, always there when the other needed them.

But why, in heaven's name, had he never realized how alluring Brenda was? How womanly? How sensual? He'd seen her in the past in a bikini that was hardly more than scraps of cloth, and it had never registered in his dumb male brain what he was actually seeing. She had just been Brenda, his best friend, whom he'd invited to come along to one of the MacAllister pool parties.

But that was then, and this was now, and he wanted her so damn much.

Don't think, MacAllister, his mind thudded. *Don't think.*

Just feel, Brenda, her mind whispered. *Don't think. Don't think.*

They kissed and caressed and explored and discovered. Where hands traveled, lips followed, and passions soared. Their breathing became quick and sharp, hearts raced and desire thrummed with ever-increasingly heated intensity within them until they could bear no more.

"Oh, Richard, please," Brenda said.

"Yes," he said, his voice a hoarse whisper.

He moved over her, then entered her, the moist heat of her femininity receiving him, welcoming all that he brought to her. He began to move, slowly at first, then increasing the tempo of the dance until it was a pounding rhythm that they matched in perfect synchronization, beat for beat. Pounding. Hotter.

Taking them higher. Then up and over the top to
fling them into oblivion seconds apart.

"Richard!"

"Bren, ah, Brenda."

They clung tightly to each other as the last waves
of ecstasy rippled through them, then they drifted
slowly back to reality.

Richard collapsed against Brenda, spent, sated,
then rolled off her with his last ounce of energy. He
tucked her close to his side, then reached down to
draw the blankets over them.

They didn't speak, each consumed with a wondrous sense of awe, of knowing that what they'd just
shared was far beyond anything they had experienced
before.

The very essence of it, the intimacy, intensity and
perfection, made it seem as though this was the first
time either of them had made love.

The complexity of their shared experience began
to inch into their minds, along with the taunting truth
that they had taken their roles of best friends to a
place where best friends didn't go.

"Don't think," Richard mumbled.

"No," Brenda said, a slight edge of panic in her
voice. "Don't think."

They gave way to the sleep that beckoned them,
gratefully, eagerly welcoming the somnolence that
claimed them, heads resting on the same pillow,
hands entwined.

Two

The ringing of a telephone, followed by an expletive mumbled in a deep voice, jolted Brenda from a deep, dreamless sleep.

She sat bolt upright on the bed, then her eyes widened as she saw Richard swing his feet to the floor and grab the receiver to the telephone on the nightstand. He remained seated on the bed, his back to Brenda.

"Hello," he said gruffly. "Yeah, I was asleep, but now I'm awake like it or not... Oh? Well, give me the details, I guess..."

Brenda snatched up the sheet to cover her nakedness and eased back onto the pillow, her mind racing as she clutched the sheet beneath her chin with both hands, her gaze riveted on Richard's broad, bare back.

Dear heaven, she thought frantically, she'd made love with Richard MacAllister! She'd shared that most intimate act with her best friend!

Oh, this was terrible, just awful. How could she have done such a thing? Richard was her chum, her buddy, her pal, her...

A soft smile formed on Brenda's lips as she shifted her gaze to the ceiling and allowed memories of the previous night to float before her mental vision.

Her lover, she mused dreamily. Never, not once in her entire twenty-six years on this planet, had she shared such incredibly beautiful lovemaking with a man.

Not that she had a whole bushel of lovers to her credit, but she knew, just somehow knew, that what had taken place between her and Richard was far and away more wondrous than the norm. It was certainly more exquisite than anything *she'd* experienced before.

They had been so perfect together, as though the magical joining had been created just for them. They had given, they had received, and it had been ecstasy. The final moment, the climax of their journey, had been nearly shattering in its intensity, had seemed to fling her into a glorious place where she had never gone before...and could only travel to with Richard.

My, my, my, what a night.

"Isn't anyone else available?" Richard said. "I just got home from Kansas City, and I'm beat, exhausted to the bone.... Yeah, I hear you, but... where's Jeff?..."

Brenda snapped out of her memory-filled haze and tightened her hold on the sheet.

Think, she told herself. She remembered how she and Richard had agreed not to think the previous night, but this was the morning after, and it was definitely time to think, think, think.

In a few moments Richard was going to end the telephone call, replace the receiver, then turn and look at her.

What was she going to say? How should she act? What would Richard say and do after what had transpired between them? She wanted to grab her pea-soup robe and hightail it to her own apartment without having said one word to Richard MacAllister.

Get a grip, Brenda, she ordered herself. She was a mature woman, who had made love with a mature man. It happened between people all the time. It was nothing to become unglued about, for Pete's sake.

Brenda closed her eyes and shook her head. Part of her was horrified at what she had done. Another part was terrified that she had destroyed a precious and rare friendship. Yet a third part was not one bit sorry that she had shared the most fantastic love-making in the world.

Oh, good grief, she thought, opening her eyes again, what was she going to say to Richard?

"Yeah, all right," Richard said. "Where will the ticket be?... You're certain there isn't a later flight that isn't booked solid? I'll really have to hustle, here.... Okay, okay. 'Bye." Richard dropped the receiver back into place. "Hell."

Mature adult, mature adult, mature adult, Brenda chanted silently, as she watch Richard turn his head slowly toward her. *I am a mature adult.*

"Hi, Bren," Richard said quietly, no readable expression on his face.

"Ohhh, I'm invisible," Brenda wailed, then pulled the sheet over her head.

Richard stretched out next to her and drew the sheet up to his armpits.

"So am I," he said, then sighed. "I'm not here, so don't attempt to speak to me."

Brenda lowered the sheet enough to peer over the top at Richard.

"Is that any way for a mature adult to behave?" she said, her words muffled slightly by the sheet. "Shame on you."

Richard rolled onto his side and propped himself on one forearm.

"But *you're* acting like a mature adult?" he said, raising his eyebrows. "Hiding under the bedclothes doesn't quite convince me, Bren."

Brenda sighed, lowered the sheet to beneath her chin and met Richard's gaze.

"I don't know what to say to you," she said. "I really don't. I'm very confused right now. All I know is that I don't want to lose you as my best friend, Richard. That would break my heart.

"What we did was wrong, I guess, because people who are best friends don't... But then again it was so beautiful, so incredible, but...we shouldn't have...but then again— Oh, I'm not making any sense."

"Yes, you are," he said, nodding. "You're echoing exactly what I would have said if you hadn't jumped in and done it first.

"I need you to be my best friend, Brenda, just as

you were before we— But you're right. What we shared was really something. It was very...beautiful, to borrow your word.

"I can't honestly say that I'm sorry we made love, but by the same token I will regret it for the rest of my life if it costs me your friendship."

Richard continued to look directly into Brenda's eyes. Desire grew between them, gaining heat, as remembrances of the previous night took front row center in their minds.

Richard jerked his head, averting his gaze, and broke the sensual spell that was beginning to weave around them.

"No, it isn't going to happen again," he said gruffly, staring at the far wall of the bedroom. "Not ever." He paused and looked at Brenda again. "Brenda, listen, okay? We've known for a long time that we're too different, poles apart on so many things, that we could never have a relationship. It just wouldn't work between us. Right?"

"Right," she said. "Wouldn't work. Nope."

"We sure make fantastic love together, though. I have never in my life experienced..." he said wistfully, then cleared his throat in the next instant. "Erase that. The issue here is our friendship, how much it means to us. Right?"

"Right," Brenda said, pressing one hand to her forehead. "Our friendship."

"Now we need to agree never to discuss what happened last night," he said slowly. "I'm thinking this through as I speak, so pay attention. Yes, that's the ticket. We won't ever talk about it.

"What we shared was awesome, it really was, but

it's over, behind us, and we're going to forget it took place. We are, at this point in time, renewing our vows as best friends.''

"Oh. Well,'' Brenda said, "that sounds reasonably reasonable…I guess. We'll just…forget it…the love-making…that was so incredibly sensual, so wonderful that it defies description and—''

"Damn it, Bren, put a cork in it,'' Richard said.

"Sorry, sorry,'' she said quickly. "I got a bit carried away there. I understand what you said, Richard. I don't know how we're going to…renew vows that I don't remember vowing in the first place but—''

"It was a figure of speech,'' he said, glowering. "We're agreeing to continue as best friends, buddies, pals, the whole nine yards. Are you with me here?''

"Absolutely,'' she said decisively. "It's an excellent plan, Richard, and I am grateful to you that you worked it all out, because my brain is mush. I hereby declare that you, Richard MacAllister, are my best friend and always will be.''

"Very good,'' he said, nodding. "I hereby declare that you, Brenda Henderson, are my best friend and always will be. And that settles that.''

"It certainly does.'' Brenda paused. "Would you please go into the living room and get my robe so I can put it on and go to my own apartment?''

"Why can't you go get the pea-soup yourself?''

"Because I don't have any clothes on, Richard,'' she said, her eyes widening. "I'm not about to parade in front of you naked as the day I was born.''

"But you want me to stroll buck naked in front of you?'' Richard shook his head. "This is ridiculous.

Our behavior is so far removed from being mature adults, it's a crime. Enough of this.''

Richard flipped back the blankets, left the bed and strode across the room.

''Oh, good heavens,'' Brenda whispered, squeezing her eyes closed. In the next instant she opened one eye to catch a glimpse of Richard. ''My, my, my.''

''You're peeking, Henderson,'' Richard said over his shoulder as he left the bedroom.

''You'd better believe it, MacAllister,'' Brenda said under her breath, then closed her eyes again.

A few moments later, the heavy, pea-soup robe landed on her head. Brenda didn't move. She heard the opening, then closing, of a dresser drawer, next the closet, then the click of the bathroom door.

When the water started to run in the shower, she slipped off the bed, shrugged into the robe, checked to see that the key to her apartment was still tucked safely in the deep pocket, then started across the room.

At the doorway to the bedroom she stopped and turned to gaze at the bed.

Richard's plan was a sound one, she thought. Neither of them wanted to do anything to jeopardize their special and rare friendship, so never discussing again what had taken place here last night was a very good idea. They would never talk about it, just go about their business as though it had never happened.

Brenda sighed and left Richard's apartment.

But she had a sneaky feeling, she thought, as she entered her own apartment a few minutes later, that it would be a very long time, if ever, before the memories of the lovemaking shared with Richard were erased from her memory.

During the next hour Brenda showered, washed and blow-dried her hair, and dressed in jeans and a red sport top. Her nearly empty cupboards and refrigerator offered little in the way of breakfast, so she consumed a bowl of cereal, sans milk, a glass of orange juice and a slice of bologna.

She was on the mend from her sinus infection, she realized, as she sat at the kitchen table. The antibiotics had apparently kicked in and done their job. She was a new woman.

She plunked one elbow on the table, rested her chin in her hand and stared into space.

Well, she thought, she was a *different* woman from the one who had sat at this table yesterday morning, which seemed like an eternity ago. She could now be counted among those who had experienced lovemaking as it—she just somehow knew—was really meant to be.

How terribly sad, she thought with a sigh to echo that sentiment, that she might very well never experience that kind of ecstasy again in her entire life.

She certainly wasn't going to make love with Richard again, and the chances of being intimate with another man sometime in the future were extremely remote.

"That rotten bum," she said aloud. "Now no one will ever be able to measure up to what I shared with Richard, and it's all his fault."

Stop it, Brenda, she ordered herself as she got to her feet. She carried her bowl and glass to the dishwasher and put them inside. She was flunking mature adult again.

None of what had transpired last night was just Richard's fault. They shared equal responsibility for what they had done, and had mutually agreed how to handle their actions' aftermath in the light of the new day.

Richard would continue with his mission to find the woman of his dreams, his soul mate, the mother of his future children. And she, she supposed, would keep going out with somebody's cousin's friend—excluding dentists—in the hope of falling in love with Mr. Right and living happily ever after.

"Right?" she said, wandering into the living room. "Right."

Brenda sank onto the sofa and propped her bare feet on the coffee table in front of it.

Why, she wondered, frowning, was the image of Richard in bed with a faceless woman causing a knot to tighten painfully in her stomach and a chill to course through her?

She didn't know, but it certainly didn't make sense. Richard would go on with his life just as it had been before they'd made love. He planned to forget what had transpired between them, never to talk about it.

And that was how it should be.

He would do his thing, she would do hers, and they'd meet in the middle as best friends, just as they'd always been.

So be it. Fine. But if that was so hunky-dory, why did she feel as if she was a breath away from bursting into tears?

Maybe she wasn't over her sinus infection, after all, she thought, pressing one hand to her cheek, her forehead, then her other cheek. She was in a weakened physical state that was rendering her emotionally wobbly.

Now *that* made sense.

"Very good," she said, getting to her feet.

She had a busy day ahead, she thought, planting one fingertip on her chin. She'd make a list and go to the grocery store. That chore completed, she'd gather her laundry and head for the basement to square off against the clothes-eating washing machines. Then later, once her clean laundry was put away, she would vacuum and dust the apartment.

"Ohhh, blak," she said, throwing up her hands. "What a gruesome way to spend a Sunday."

A brisk knock sounded at the door and Brenda crossed the room, opened the door and stared up at a frowning Richard, who was wearing jeans and a black knit shirt.

"Tacky," he said gruffly. He strode past her, then turned to face her in the middle of the room. "To leave my bed and disappear while I was in the shower was very tacky, Bren."

"Why?" she said, closing the door. "You knew I was coming over here as soon as I had my peasoup."

"There's certain etiquette involved in the morning after, Ms. Henderson," he said, folding his arms over his chest. "Splitting the scene while I was in the shower would not cut it with Miss Manners."

"Miss Manners doesn't deal with this stuff," Brenda said, matching Richard's pose. "Well, I don't think she does. But the point is, we were beyond the morning after, Mr. MacAllister. We'd thoroughly discussed it and reached the agreement never to discuss it…or whatever. So as far as your grumpy mood goes—get over it.''

Richard sighed and dragged a hand through his hair.

''I'm sorry,'' he said. ''You're right. The morning after was a done deal. I'm just bummed because I have to fly to Detroit in two hours. That would be fine if I was in the market for a new car, but I'm not, so I sure as hell don't feel like going to Detroit.''

''You're leaving again? So soon?'' Brenda said, sitting down on the sofa. ''They usually give you at least a few days to recuperate and tend to your personal business between assignments.''

''Yeah, I know,'' he said, slouching onto a chair opposite the sofa. ''This is an emergency that's more of an emergency than usual, and no one else is available.''

''But what about your sister's wedding, Richard?'' Brenda said. ''She and Andrew are getting married next weekend. You can't miss Kara's wedding. What if the job in Detroit isn't finished by then?''

''I'll keep in touch with Kara if the job runs that long,'' he said, ''and see if they're going to have to postpone the ceremony again. If it's going to take place this weekend, I'll fly in for the wedding, then go back to Detroit if it comes to that. They've pushed the date back twice already so…'' He shrugged.

''That wasn't their fault,'' Brenda said. ''Kara and Andrew have their hearts set on getting married in the living room of their new home that's being built.

The unseasonable rains we had kept creating delays in the construction. Now there's some kind of snafu with the delivery of the carpeting they ordered. I really don't know if they'll be able to get married next weekend or not.''

"Yeah, well, like I said, I'll call Kara from Detroit.'' Richard paused. "Do you...um...have a date lined up to go to the wedding with you?''

"No,'' Brenda said, shaking her head. "The wedding is for family only, and I'm very honored to think I'm considered among that number. I wouldn't dream of inviting anyone else to go with me.''

Richard nodded. "So, why don't we go together when they finally do the deed?''

"Sure. That's fine. Besides, we pooled our money to buy them the propane barbecue that's wrapped and ready in your spare bedroom. We really should accompany our mutual gift.''

"Good,'' Richard said, getting to his feet. "That's settled then. I've got to pack and get to the airport. How are you feeling? You know, your sinus infection?''

Brenda stood. "I think I'm cured. Maybe.'' She laughed. "I might convince myself that I'll have a relapse if I go to the grocery store, then do my laundry and clean the apartment, though. That's what's on my exciting agenda for today.''

"Beats flying to Detroit. Well, I've got to shove off.'' Richard didn't move. "Yep, gotta go.''

"Okay. 'Bye. Have a nice flight. I'll see you when you get back. 'Bye, Richard.''

"Goodbye, Bren,'' Richard said, still not moving. Their eyes met, held, and hearts began to increase their tempo. Richard took one step toward Brenda at the exact same moment that she took one step toward him. Richard blinked, cleared his throat to break the sensual spell, then strode toward the door.

"See ya," he said, then left the apartment, closing the door behind him with more force than was necessary.

"See ya," Brenda whispered to the empty room, then sniffled as unwelcomed and unexplainable tears filled her eyes.

Three

"Well, Brenda, you are most definitely...pregnant."

Dr. Kara MacAllister folded her hands on top of a medical file and looked intently at Brenda, who was sitting in a chair opposite the desk in Kara's office.

"Brenda?" Kara said, raising her eyebrows.

"Oh," Brenda said. "I was waiting for you to finish the joke, Kara. Actually you didn't start it quite right. You're supposed to say, 'Mrs. Henderson, I have good news for you,' then I say, 'It's *Miss* Henderson,' then you deliver the punch line by ending with, 'Miss Henderson, I have *bad* news for you.'"

Brenda shrugged. "That's okay. I'm lousy at telling jokes, too." She paused. "So! What's wrong with me? Why have I been feeling so tired and having so many upset tummies lately?

"Oh, before I forget, thank you for seeing me today. I booked a cruise for the doctor I've had since I was born and he's off to…wherever it is that I sent him. I can't keep all of my client's destinations straight in my mind."

"Brenda," Kara said, leaning back in her chair, "I wasn't attempting to tell a joke. You…really…are…pregnant. You're about four weeks along, and that is why you've been tired and suffering from morning sickness, which in your case is apparently lasting most of the day."

Brenda opened her mouth, closed it, then leaned forward in her chair.

"Pardon me?" she said. "I'm four weeks… what?"

"Pregnant," Kara said. "With child. Have a bun in the oven." She threw up her hands. "How many ways do you want me to say this?"

Brenda jumped to her feet. "That's impossible. I certainly am not pregnant, Kara MacAllister. How can you suggest such a thing? You've made a mistake. I realize that you and Andrew are finally getting married tomorrow after a zillion delays, but you really must keep your mind on your work while you're in your doctor mode. You goofed, Kara, but I forgive you."

"Brenda, please, sit down."

Brenda sank back onto the chair. "I'm on the Pill, remember? One does not get pregnant when one is on the Pill, Dr. MacAllister."

"Yes, one does, Ms. Henderson," Kara said, "when one takes antibiotics that override the effect of birth control pills. You told me that you were on

antibiotics for a sinus infection a month ago, and,
putting that information together with your cy-
cle…plus the test I ran and the examination I did…
How much more evidence do you need? You're going to have a baby.''

"Don't be silly." Brenda's eyes widened in the
next instant and her stomach dropped. *"I'm going to
have a baby?"*

"Finally," Kara said, her shoulders slumping with
relief. "I got through to you. Yes, my sweet friend,
you're going to have a baby.''

Kara got to her feet and rounded the desk. She
turned a second chair toward Brenda, sat down, then
grasped both of Brenda's hands in hers.

"You obviously didn't entertain the thought that
you might be pregnant, did you?" Kara said gently.

"No," Brenda said, her widened eyes riveted on
Kara. "I don't believe this. Well, I mean, I believe
it, but…I don't believe this!''

Kara released Brenda's hands, patted her on the
knee, then leaned back in the chair.

"Well, it's true, Brenda," she said. "You don't
have to make any decisions today regarding this
pregnancy, but you are certainly aware, I'm sure, that
there are several options open to you. Of course,
there's also the opinion of the baby's father to be
considered, should you choose to tell him about
this.''

"The…baby's…father?" Brenda whispered.
Richard. Oh, dear heaven, she was pregnant with
Richard MacAllister's baby. "I don't believe this.''

Kara laughed. "You're starting to sound like a
broken record." She became serious again in the

next moment. "Bren, please don't take offense at this question, but I have to ask it. Do you know who the father is?"

"Oh, yes, I know who he is," Brenda said. "I don't exactly have a long string of lovers beating down my door, Kara." She sighed. "Good grief, what a mess, what a disaster, what a catastrophe, what a—"

"Cut," Kara said, slicing one hand through the air. "I get the point. You're not thrilled down to your toes that you're going to have a baby."

Brenda splayed both hands on her flat stomach. A soft smile formed on her lips.

"A baby," she said, awe ringing in her voice. "A miracle. Nestled within me. Growing, being nurtured, even as we speak. Isn't that incredible? I wonder if it's a girl or a boy. Oh, my stars, it's a teeny-tiny person. Kara, I'm a mother-to-be. I'm going to have a baby."

"Really?" Kara said, laughing again. "Well, I guess that settles the question of whether or not you're planning to keep this child. Yes?"

"Oh, yes. Yes, of course I am," Brenda said. "I'm so excited. No, actually, I'm terrified." She waved one hand in the air. "Ignore all that. I just need time to get used to the idea, that's all, then I can cancel the terrified…I hope."

"Those mixed emotions are very understandable." Kara paused. "Let's move back to the subject of the father, shall we?"

"Oh, let's not," Brenda said, shaking her head. *It's your big brother, Richard, Kara. How about that for a newsflash?* "I don't want to discuss him."

"Why not? Don't you think he'll be supportive?"

"He'd like to be, but not to me," Brenda said. "It's very complicated, Kara, and I just don't want to get into it."

"All right…for now, but the subject of his paternity isn't going to disappear because it's… uncomfortable for you in some way. Do know that I'm here if you want to talk it through. Shall I have the test results sent over to your regular doctor's office?"

"No, I'd rather have you be my doctor from now on," Brenda said. "I know you're not taking on any new patients, because you cut back on your doctoring hours so you can have more mommying hours with Andy but, please, Kara, say you'll be my physician through this pregnancy."

"Yes, of course I will," Kara said.

"Thank you. Is Andy going to be at your wedding tomorrow?"

"Indeed, he is," Kara said, smiling. "Andrew and I bought him the cutest little suit to wear. The other great news is that I spoke with our social worker this morning, and all the documents are ready for Andrew to sign to adopt Andy just as soon as the wedding takes place. We'll all be Malones, although I'll keep the name MacAllister professionally. It's less confusing for my patients that way.

"And we're getting off the subject of *your* baby's father by chatting about *my* baby's father," Kara said. "I know you don't want to talk about your baby's daddy, but since you plan to keep this child, don't you think the man has a right to know that he's going to be a father?"

"No. Yes. Well, I guess so," Brenda said, frowning. "Yes, I suppose he'll have to be told."

Besides, Brenda thought, it would be rather impossible to hide the fact since she lived next door to the father of her baby. The father of her baby... Richard MacAllister. Oh, merciful saints, she really couldn't believe this.

One night. One. She had made love with Richard on that one night and—bingo—here she was pregnant with his baby. Just one glorious, lovemaking night and...

How on earth was she going to find the words to tell all this to Richard? He was going to pitch the fit of the century, that was for sure. She wasn't supposed to be the mother of his child; she was the designated best friend, buddy, pal and chum.

"Well," Kara said, getting to her feet and bringing Brenda from her racing thoughts. "I've got another patient waiting for me. I'm going to give you a prescription for some prenatal vitamins, plus a packet of information that I've put together for my mommies-to-be. If you have any questions, just call.

"Make an appointment to see me in a month. As for your morning sickness, there are some tips on dealing with that in the material I'm giving you."

Brenda stood, and Kara hugged her.

"Congratulations," Kara said. "I can say that, now that I know you want this baby." She placed her hands on Brenda's cheeks. "Remember this, too, Brenda. No matter how the father of your child reacts, you're not alone. You're considered a member of the MacAllister family, and you have a lot of people to stand by you and support you.

"I want you to know that, especially since your parents are not in Ventura now and you don't know when they'll return from their vacation in Greece. Your pregnancy is a confidential matter between us, but when the time comes to let it be known, the MacAllisters will all be there for you."

A nearly hysterical bubble of laughter escaped from Brenda's lips.

"Did I miss something?" Kara said, dropping her hands from Brenda's cheeks.

"No, no. It's an inside joke." Brenda closed her eyes and shook her head. "I really wish I hadn't said that." She opened her eyes again. "Well, I'll see you at your wedding tomorrow. You're absolutely, positively certain that you're getting married tomorrow afternoon, aren't you?"

Kara laughed. "Yes. Everyone has been so patient with our ongoing delays, one after the other. But the big day has finally arrived. Andrew and I are being married in the living room of our beautiful new home, just as we wanted to be. It's perfect."

"Well," Brenda said, picking an imaginary thread from the skirt of her dress, "I guess Richard must be winging his way home from Detroit by now so he'll be able to attend the ceremony."

"He'd better be if he wants to live to celebrate his next birthday," Kara said. "I've got to dash. Stop at the desk on the way out to make an appointment and get your goodies from Lucy, the receptionist. See you tomorrow, Brenda."

Wishing Well Travel Agency, the thriving business that Brenda managed for the globe-trotting

owner, was located in one of the popular shopping
malls in Ventura.

To Brenda's utmost relief she'd been able to blank
her mind and concentrate totally on the heavy traffic
as she drove back to the agency after seeing Kara
and receiving what she mentally referred to as The
Newsflash.

Once inside the temperature-controlled mall, however, the full impact of The Newsflash had seemed
to slam against her. She'd sat on a wooden bench
next to a fountain, her trembling legs refusing to support her for one more second.

She was going to have a baby, she thought frantically. And not just any baby. No, not her. She was
going to have her best friend's baby, a child con-
ceived with Richard MacAllister.

Brenda looked at the people who were bustling
past her, wondering why they weren't staring at her.
Surely the fact that she was newly pregnant was ra-
diating from her like a neon sign. She certainly felt
different, not remotely close to who she had been
when she had gotten out of bed that morning.

Nope, she thought, as more people hurried by, that
group hadn't paid the least bit of attention to her
either. So, okay, her secret was a secret...for now.

But how long would it be before she looked like
someone attempting to smuggle a basketball? How
long could she postpone telling Richard that she was
pregnant with his baby?

She sighed. She was so tired, just thoroughly exhausted. Even the hard wooden bench she was
perched on was tempting her to curl up on it and
take a nap.

But she couldn't sleep...she had to think. Richard would no doubt be flying in from Detroit this evening to be on hand for Kara and Andrew's wedding tomorrow. She hadn't heard word one from him since he left for Detroit a month ago, the day after the night they'd made love....

Don't go there, Brenda, she told herself. She'd spent the past four weeks dragging her mind back from the sensual memories of the lovemaking shared with Richard. That she would never forget that night was a given. Her goal now was to go an entire day without thinking about the ecstasy of what had happened between them.

Well, she didn't have time for *that* mental tug-of-war. She was probably only hours away from being face-to-face with Richard. She had to decide right this minute what she was going to do about The Newsflash.

Tell Richard about the baby as soon as she saw him?

Wait until she was no longer capable of hiding the basketball?

Move to Siberia and forget she ever knew Richard MacAllister?

"Get a grip, Brenda," she said aloud.

"Yeah, Brenda, get a grip," a teenager said, as he strolled past her. "You're losing it."

"I know," she said, then realized the boy, who was a complete stranger to her, was well beyond where she was sitting.

She shook her head in self-disgust and got to her feet. She had two more hours to work, then she'd head home, have some dinner and wait for Richard to pound on the wall and announce that he had arrived at his apartment.

Then what? she asked herself, as she made her way through the crowd. She didn't have a clue. She would just wait and see what popped out of her mouth when she actually saw Richard in living, breathing Technicolor.

No, she decided, as she entered the travel agency, that was a wishy-washy plan. She had to get it together, be decisive, act like the ever-famous mature adult she supposedly was.

"Hi, Brenda," one of the agents, a man in his midthirties said, as she wandered by his desk. "Did the doc tell you what you wanted to know?"

Brenda stopped and spun around.

"What?" she said. "Who said I wanted to know something from a doctor, Kevin?"

"*You* did," Kevin said, frowning. "You said you had a doc appointment because you wanted to know what was making you feel tired all the time."

"Oh. Yes. I said that, didn't I?" she said, nodding. "Well, I know what's making me feel tired all the time, all right."

"No kidding?" Kevin said. "Is it— Gosh, Bren, is it really serious? Are you about to cry? Should *I* get ready to cry?"

Brenda laughed. "No, Kevin, you don't have to prepare yourself to cry, but I appreciate your willingness to weep buckets for me. I'm fine, really. I just have a teeny-tiny problem caused by the antibiotics I took when I had my sinus infection. In time—" eight more months to be precise "—I'll be as good as new."

"Well, great," Kevin said, smiling. "Glad to hear it." The telephone on his desk rang, and he picked up the receiver. "Wishing Well Travel Agency. This is Kevin. How may I help you?"

I'm beyond help, Brenda thought, continuing across the room and entering her office.

She put her purse in the bottom drawer of her desk, then sank onto the leather chair.

A plan, she thought. She needed a definite plan of action in regard to telling Richard about the baby. So. Okay. The plan is…

"Is?" She opened her hands in front of her as though a plan would drop into them from the heavens. "Is? Well, darn it."

She propped an elbow on the top of her desk and rested her chin in her palm, staring off into space.

Richard was flying in from Detroit to attend Kara and Andrew's wedding. Check.

She had no idea if he was home to stay for a while, or if he'd have to return to Detroit immediately following the festive event. Check.

She and Richard had decided weeks before to attend the wedding together, along with the propane barbecue present. Check.

The MacAllisters were intelligent and caring people, who would pick up in a second on any strain or stress between her and Richard. Therefore, it would not be a good idea to tell Richard about The Newsflash before the ceremony, regardless of whether he was going back to Detroit or not. Check.

So, okay, she would divulge The Newsflash to Richard when they were safely back in her apartment after the wedding. Then she'd hope to the heavens that he was flying out to Detroit where he could get used to The Newsflash, leaving her in peace to come to grips with it herself. Check.

"Hooray!" she said. "I have a plan."

"No," Kevin said, poking his head into her office. "You have a call on line three. Mrs. Gillispie wants to know if you made reservations for her pit bull's stay at the Doggy Dude Ranch while she and Mr. G. are in Europe."

"The Doggy Dude Ranch won't take pit bulls," Brenda said. "Say, Kevin, how would you like to baby-sit a darling little pit bull while—"

"I'm gone," he said.

"Well, cripe," Brenda said, reaching for the telephone receiver.

Early the next afternoon Brenda set her purse and a tote bag on the sofa and stared at the far wall of the living room with narrowed eyes, willing it to produce the sound of three solid thumps.

Where on earth was Richard? she thought, beginning to pace back and forth. She'd fallen asleep on the sofa last evening, clad in her comforting pea-soup robe, having spent long, nerve-racking hours waiting for Richard's thunks on the wall that never came. Now there was only about an hour left before it would be time to leave to go to Kara and Andrew's house for the wedding. Why wasn't Richard home?

She sighed and pressed one hand against her stomach that felt as it had the one and only time she'd gone on a roller coaster.

Morning sickness twenty-four hours a day was the pits, she thought, sinking onto the sofa. The material that Kara had given her suggested that a mother-to-be who was suffering from morning sickness nibble on saltine crackers. If she ate one more cracker, she was going to burst, and she still felt yucky.

"Blak," she said, then smoothed the skirt of the pretty mint-green dress she'd bought especially for this occasion.

Her exhausted mind, she decided, leaning her head back on the top of the sofa, was all over the place. One minute she was thrilled to pieces about the prospect of having a baby, the next, scared to death at being a single mother, and always she dreaded the moment when she had to tell Richard she was pregnant with his baby.

She just wanted to go to the wedding and have a wonderful time with people she adored. She was going to, somehow, push The Newsflash to the back of her brain and thoroughly enjoy herself at the MacAllister gathering. And she would not say a word to Richard about The Newsflash before the wedding.

But if Richard didn't hurry up and arrive at his apartment, he wouldn't even be at the ceremony for her to tell him.

Brenda frowned. "Huh? Did that make sense?"

Well, she knew what she meant. Where was Richard, for heaven's sake?

Three loud knocks sounded on the far wall, causing Brenda to gasp in surprise at the sudden noise. She jumped to her feet, swallowed heavily as her tummy objected to the abrupt motion, then hurried to the wall to give it two whacks, which were answered by one thump.

"Okay, this is it," Brenda said, nodding. "Richard

is home and wants me to come over. I'll just act normally, be chipper and upbeat. I can handle this. No problem.''

She grabbed her purse and tote bag from the sofa and sooner than she would have preferred she was rapping on Richard's apartment door. Richard opened the door, then turned immediately and began to walk across the living room, leaving Brenda standing out in the hallway.

''Come on in, Bren,'' he said over one shoulder. ''I have to be in front of a mirror to do my tie.'' He disappeared into the bedroom.

Brenda entered the apartment and closed the door behind her.

In his bedroom Richard stared at his reflection in the mirror above the chest of drawers. Brenda looked beautiful, he thought, really lovely. Her dress was the color of pistachio ice cream, her hair was fluttering around her face in soft, silky waves and—

Get a grip, MacAllister, Richard ordered himself, as he began to tie his tie. Damn, this had been a long month. A month filled with images of Brenda and memories of the incredible lovemaking they'd shared. He'd done one lousy job of erasing their fantastic night together from his mind. Really lousy.

He'd replayed what they'd shared over and over in his mental vision until he'd been ready to holler the roof down with frustration over not being able to forget what had happened.

Well, he was home now, having put in tediously long hours to complete the assignment in Detroit at long last. He'd be able to view Brenda in the proper manner again. She was his best friend. That was it.

Pure and simple. The way it had always been and always would be.

"Got it," he said, nodding at his reflection.

He strode from the room and entered the living room to find Brenda standing just inside the door.

"Hey, make yourself comfortable," he said, stopping in the middle of the room. "We don't have to leave for a while yet. Sit. I'll get the wedding present and be right back. Did you bring your bathing suit? Oh, yeah, you have your tote bag. We're going to christen Kara and Andrew's new pool after they get hitched. This should be a great party, don't you think?"

Richard spun around and left the room.

Brenda took a much-needed deep breath and walked forward to sink onto the sofa.

She'd forgotten to breathe, she thought, taking another long breath. She'd just stared at Richard as though she'd never seen him before in her life. She'd been viewing him, she realized, not as her buddy, but as the father of her child. The whole concept was so strange, new and foreign that she'd failed to inhale then exhale, finally causing little black dots to dance before her eyes.

But she was fine now. Had her act together. She was in control. Richard was the same ol' Richard. Granted, he looked like a million dollars in his tan suit and dark brown shirt and… But no big deal. He was always handsome as all get-out, because he was a very handsome-as-all-get-out man and…and she was mentally babbling like a nutcase.

Richard returned with the huge present that was

wrapped in paper with silver bells and doves as a design. He set the gift on a chair.

"That's heavy," he said, then smiled at Brenda. "How are you? I'm late getting in because we got stacked up above Denver, but I made it with time to spare. I'm showered, shaved and spit shined. Hey, want to hear some trivia from Detroit?"

Richard sat down on his favorite lumpy recliner.

"Okay, here we go," he said. "Motown trivia. Brenda, my pal, did you know that a shark is the only fish that can blink with both eyes? How's that? Dynamite, huh? I have another one, too. Ready? There are more chickens than people in the world."

Richard punched one fist in the air.

"Yes!" he said. "Great stuff. You're going to have to go a stretch to beat those, Bren. I really out-did myself this time. So? What have you got for me? Lay some new trivia on your buddy, here."

"Richard," Brenda said, then promptly burst into tears. "Richard, I'm...I'm pregnant...with your baby."

Four

Brenda blinked away her tears and stared at Richard, who was staring at her.

The emotions displayed on Richard's face, Brenda realized, were changing so fast it was like an old-fashioned slide show…click…another one came into view. If it wasn't for the fact that The Newsflash was causing Richard such obvious confusion and turmoil, it would be fascinating to watch.

The first expression she'd seen register on Richard's face had been rather smug, as though she was kidding around and he'd figured that out immediately, a "Yeah, right, Bren" expression.

Then he exhibited openmouthed incredulity, then his mouth snapped closed, accompanied by a sharp shake of his head indicating disbelief, then his eyes widened with the realization that what she had announced was true.

And now...what was this? A smile was tugging Richard's lips? No, certainly not. But...yes, he was smiling and it was growing bigger, becoming a full-blown grin.

Oh, poor Richard. He'd gone right over the edge of his sanity because of The Newsflash. He was sitting there grinning like a fool.

"We're...we're going to have a baby?" Richard said, getting to his feet, the smile still firmly in place. "That is so fantastic, so..." He frowned. "But I thought you were on the Pill." The smile slowly returned to his face. "A baby."

"Richard, for heaven's sake," Brenda said, "get a grip, would you? This is not a smiling matter. Read my lips. I...am...pregnant. Me. Your buddy, your pal, your chum Brenda. The antibiotics I was taking for that sinus infection nullified the birth control pills."

"That's rather fascinating trivia," Richard said thoughtfully. "Antibiotics can override the medically proven capabilities of birth control pills and—"

"Richard!" Brenda said, jumping to her feet. "This is not part of our yearlong trivia game. This is real. I'm going to have our baby. Me." She splayed both hands on her breasts. "Your best friend."

A smiling Richard nodded.

"Would you quit grinning like an idiot?" Brenda yelled. "Are you in shock? That's it, isn't it?" Fresh tears filled her eyes and she sniffled. "I'm trying to communicate with a zombie," she said, throwing up her hands. "I'm taking my baby and going to the wedding. Goodbye, Richard."

"Bren, wait." Richard closed the distance between them and gripped Brenda's shoulders. "I've heard every word you've said, I swear it. I was rather stunned at first and a tad terrified, I admit that, but I definitely know that this…this…"

"The Newsflash," Brenda interrupted. "That's what I call it…with capital letters." She sniffled again.

"Okay, The Newsflash. I know The Newsflash is real." Richard took a handkerchief from his back pocket and gave it to Brenda.

"I can't find the other handkerchief you loaned me," she said, dabbing at her nose. "I think the washing machine ate it."

"Don't worry about it," he said. "What's mine is yours. Literally. Everything." He framed Brenda's face with his hands. "Listen to me, please? I know you're upset, and I'm sorry that I wasn't here with you when you found out about…about The Newsflash. But, Brenda? We're going to be fine, just fine, you'll see. We'll get married right away and—"

Brenda's eyes widened and she took a step backward, forcing Richard to drop his hands from her face.

"Married? Married!" she said, none too quietly. "That's the craziest thing I've ever heard. We're not in love with each other, remember? We're just best friends, remember? We are not getting married, Richard."

"Tell that to Flash, there," he said, pointing to her stomach. "He has a mother and a father who both want him and— You do want him, don't you, Bren?''

"Of course I do," she said. "How can you even ask me such a thing?"

"So, okay, then it's settled. We both want our baby, so we'll get married and—''

"No! No! No!" Brenda said, pressing her fingertips to her now-throbbing temples. "Richard, please, just slow down and think. We knew within twenty-four hours of meeting each other that we were exact opposites. We're totally incompatible people, don't you see?

"As best friends we're terrific, top-of-the-line. But as husband and wife living under the same roof? That thought is enough to give me cold chills. It wouldn't work, Richard, it just wouldn't. We'd end up despising each other. Besides, I don't intend to marry anyone unless I'm deeply in love with him and he returns that love in kind."

"Oh." Richard frowned and hooked one hand over the back of his neck as he stared at the floor, digesting what Brenda had said. He dropped his hand heavily to his side and looked at her again. "Well, hell, Bren, I want to be a part of my child's life, be the best father possible. Being a weekend daddy like the majority of my divorced men friends just isn't going to cut it for me."

"It won't be like that," Brenda said, shaking her head. "I mean, heavens, we live right next door to each other. You could see the baby whenever you wished."

"Oh, yeah? And how do we explain this weird arrangement to our child?" he said.

Brenda sighed wearily. "I'm only four weeks pregnant. We've got a great deal of time before our son, or daughter, requires an explanation as to our lifestyle. I'm still getting used to the idea that I'm going to have a baby, without taking on the worries connected to the psyche of this child down the road. One step at a time. Okay?

"The first thing on the agenda is getting to Kara and Andrew's wedding. We've got to leave now, or we're going to be late."

"Maybe we could get a group discount from the minister today," Richard said, smiling. "A two-for-the-price-of-one deal. He can marry us after he does his thing for Kara and Andrew."

"Richard, we are *not* getting married. Just erase that from your mind because it isn't going to happen. Not now, not later, not ever."

"Mmm," he said, shoving his hands into his trouser pockets.

"Oh, and one other thing. Please don't tell anyone about the baby at this MacAllister event we're about to attend. I need some private time with The Newsflash before it becomes known to your whole family. Kara knows because she's the one who told *me* that I was pregnant, but she won't divulge it."

"I bet she tells Andrew," Richard said, narrowing his eyes. "A husband and wife shouldn't have any secrets from each other."

"She can't tell him," Brenda said. "It falls under patient and doctor confidentiality. The important thing today is that you act normally, behave like you always would around me. Your family will pick up on any stress between us in a heartbeat."

"I'm not stressed," he said, grinning at her, though his eyes conveyed an inner turmoil. "I'm going to be a daddy."

"Well, *I'm* stressed, okay? Besides that, I have morning sickness that can't tell time. It just hangs around twenty-four hours a day."

Richard stepped forward and wrapped his arms around Brenda. She stiffened, then decided to indulge in the comforting warmth and strength of Richard…just for a moment.

"I'm so sorry you don't feel well," he said, as she rested her head on his broad chest. "Can't Kara do something about it?"

"I'm supposed to eat saltine crackers."

"We'll stop on the way to the wedding and get some," he said decisively. "A whole bunch. A couple dozen boxes of saltine crackers."

"I have plenty, thank you. They don't work. Hopefully this all-day morning sickness won't last too long. We've got to leave, Richard, or we'll be late, and that isn't fair to Kara and Andrew."

"We're on our way," he said, not moving.

They stood perfectly still, close, arms entwined around each other, each lost in their own thoughts, each sifting the realization of The Newsflash, their baby, through their minds, hearts and souls, soft smiles of wonder and awe forming on their lips.

Then memories of the exquisite lovemaking they'd shared weeks before began to creep in around the edges of their minds, and desire began to hum within them, gaining force and heat with each beat of their hearts.

"Mmm," Brenda said dreamily.

"Whew," Richard said, then slowly, reluctantly, eased Brenda away from his body and kissed her gently on the forehead. "We'd better get it in gear here."

Brenda blinked, then nodded.

"There's something I need to say to you, Bren," Richard said, his voice slightly husky. "It doesn't seem adequate, isn't enough to express how I feel, but...thank you. You're giving me the greatest gift I've ever had. My child. We sure didn't plan on this happening, but I...well, thank you, Brenda."

Brenda nodded, unable to speak as her throat closed with tears.

"Hi, Aunt Brenda," a child's voice said. "Aren't you goin' to go swimming with us?"

Brenda opened her eyes, then sat up in the lounge chair and smiled at the three identical little girls clad in rainbow-colored bathing suits.

"Hello, Jessica, Emily and Alice MacAllister," Brenda said. "You look cute as buttons in your suits."

"Where's your bathing suit, Aunt Brenda?" one of the girls said.

"I have it on under this swim robe," Brenda said. "I'm just too lazy to go into the pool today. I decided to just lie here in the sun and relax." Truth be told, she had the ridiculous notion that everyone gathered would know in a second that she was pregnant if she paraded around in her bikini. "So! Lovely triplets of Forrest and Jillian, how do you like being six years old?"

"It's good," one of the girls said, nodding. "It's

better than being five was, 'cause we get to stay up fifteen minutes later at night.''

''Aunt Brenda,'' another one of the trio said, ''how come you cried so much at Aunt Kara and Uncle Andrew's wedding in the house? I heard you get the hiccups and stuff. Are you so very, very sad that Aunt Kara and Uncle Andrew got married?''

''Oh, no…which triplet are you?'' Brenda said, frowning.

''I'm Jessica.''

''No, Jessica,'' Brenda said, ''I wasn't sad.'' It's like this, kiddo. According to the information Kara gave me, my pregnant hormones are all whacked and I cry at the drop of a hat. Plus, well, sweetie, Kara and Andrew are obviously so much in love and I guess I was feeling a bit lonely and a lot scared about this baby I'm going to have and… ''It was all so special and wonderful, Jessica, that I got tears in my eyes, that's all.''

''A whole bunch of tears,'' Jessica said.

''Yes, well…'' Brenda said. ''Don't you want to get into that beautiful new swimming pool? Maybe I'll join you later. Okay?''

'''Kay,'' the three girls said in unison, then ran toward the sparkling blue water.

Brenda sank back on the lounge, closed her eyes again and sighed.

We'll get married right away.

Richard's words echoed yet again in Brenda's mind and she mentally pleaded with them to go away and leave her alone.

Marrying Richard MacAllister was not up for consideration. When he calmed down and thought it through, he'd realize that he was lucky that she hadn't snapped up his offer and put a date for their wedding in her day-planner…in ink.

In all fairness, she thought, she had to give Richard credit for being wonderful about The Newsflash. He hadn't raged in anger, nor roared in denial, nor acted like a cornered man who was being forced into the role of father, which he wanted no part of.

No, not Richard. He was tickled pink about the whole thing, was ready to march her off to city hall and put a ring on her finger. That was very sweet, but it wasn't going to happen. No. No way. She had no intention of marrying a man who didn't love her and whom she didn't love in return.

Well, she loved Richard, couldn't imagine life without him, but it was best-buddy love, not romantic love. Then again, that night they'd shared, the one incredible lovemaking night, had been romantic to the max, but that had just sort of…happened.

It was not the stuff of which marriages made in heaven were based on. Not even close. Baby or not, she was not pledging forever to a man who was nothing more than her best friend.

Brenda sniffled.

Oh, darn it, she fumed, she was going to cry again. Why was she getting weepy now? She didn't know, didn't have a clue, but at this rate she was going to spend the next eight months with a red nose and a clogged-sinus headache to go along with the all-day-long morning sickness.

"Hey, Flash, aren't you coming into the pool?"

Brenda's eyes flew open as Richard sat down on the lounge next to her.

"Richard, hush," she said, looking quickly around. "Don't call me that. Someone will hear you."

"They wouldn't think anything of it," he said, smiling. "They'd just figure it's a new nickname I've given you. I think it's cute, very clever, a secret code for The Newsflash, Flash." He paused. "Why are you all bundled up in that robe?"

Brenda sat up and tightened the sash on the terry cloth cover-up.

"I don't know," she said. "I just feel...strange, like my body isn't mine, or something. I had this nutsy thought that everyone would be able to tell that—" She glanced around again. "You know what I mean." She sighed. "Richard, I'd like to go home as soon as it's politely possible. I really need some time alone."

"Well, sure, Bren, we can leave whenever you want to," he said, reaching over and taking one of her hands in his. "Just say the word and we're gone."

"No, that's not fair to you, Richard," Brenda said. "I'll say I have a headache and call a taxi. You stay here. This party will go on for hours yet, and there's no reason for you to miss out on the fun."

"Not a chance," Richard said. "I brought you, I'll see you safely home. Besides, how could I enjoy myself if I know you're all alone in your apartment? You might even be crying. You've done a lot of that today. Nope. If you want to go home, I'll take you."

"That doesn't make sense," she said, leaning toward him. "I want some private time. That means you'd be sitting in your own apartment staring at the walls, when you could be here having fun with your family.''

"No, I'd be with you in your apartment. I wouldn't talk to you or anything, just read a magazine, watch the tube. You could have all the privacy you needed, just pretend I'm not there. You're not yourself today, Bren, which is understandable. I couldn't play touch football later, while I knew you were curled up on your sofa probably wearing your pea-soup because you're upset, or whatever it is that you are.''

"Ohhh,'' Brenda said, sinking back on the lounge. "You don't understand the definition of private time, Richard MacAllister.''

"Private time,'' a new voice said, "as defined by a woman is a very complicated thing.''

"And I suppose you're an all-fired expert on the subject, Cousin Michael,'' Richard said, frowning.

"Indeed, I am, Cousin Richard,'' Michael said, pulling a lawn chair next to Brenda's lounge and sitting down. "I am a man of vast knowledge regarding the strange workings of women's minds.''

"This ought to be enlightening,'' Brenda said, peering at Michael with one eye. "Go for it, Michael.''

"I intend to,'' Michael said. "Okay, Richard, listen up. When a woman says she wants to have some private time, you disappear, leave her alone.''

"Amen,'' Brenda said, closing her eye again.

"However,'' Michael continued, raising one finger, "don't go too far away, because you are definitely expected to be there if said woman has a sudden thought she wishes to discuss with you that has come to her while she is having her private time.

"In other words, hover unseen in the shadows. There's no heading for a ball game or the local pub, my boy, because that gets you in very deep trouble." He nodded. "I have spoken."

Brenda opened her eyes and laughed. "Good grief, Michael, you make women sound like fruitcakes."

"Hey, am I right or not, Bren?" Michael said. "I nailed it, I know I did."

"Well, yes, sort of…I guess," Brenda said slowly. "But you're talking about you and Jenny. You two are married and…Richard doesn't have to get a handle on the intricacies of *my* private-time request. We're best friends, not husband and wife."

"But you're forgetting something important, Brenda," Michael said, getting to his feet. "Yes, Jenny and I are married, have been for quite a few years now. But what I don't think you realize is that Jenny is also my best friend and vice versa. Think about it. It's very important. See you later."

Brenda frowned as she watched Michael walk away, then shifted her gaze to Richard.

"Did that last bit of his make sense?" she said.

"Not really." Richard shrugged. "Forget it. Michael blithers on at times just to hear the sound of his own voice." He paused. "Look, I'll do whatever you want me to about your private-time thing. Your call."

Brenda smiled. "I'll stay here at the party."

"Are you sure you want to?"

"Yes, I'm positive," she said. "I'll even cheer for you when you play touch football later. Thank you,

Richard, for being willing to go home with me. That was very sweet of you and I appreciate it.''

''Hey, what are best friends for?'' Richard frowned. ''What they're not supposed to do is bring The Newsflash into your life. Bren, have I messed up here? Should I be apologizing to you, asking you to forgive me for what has happened?''

''No, Richard,'' Brenda said, smiling at him warmly. ''We were both there, equal partners in— Well, enough said.'' She swung her feet to the grass. ''I'm finished with this silly business of sitting here covered up like a mummy. Come on, let's go swimming.''

Late that night Richard cut loose with a string of earthy expletives as he left his bed, smoothed the sheets, tucked in the edges, pounded on the pillow, then flopped back down.

He was punchy from lack of sleep, he thought, would never recover from his jet lag if he didn't quit tossing and turning and demolishing his bed.

But he just couldn't shut off his mind, kept dwelling on the fact that he was going to be a father, that Brenda was carrying his baby.

The Newsflash was really sinking in, hitting him like a ton of bricks, causing a never-ending jumble of questions to chase each other around in his brain.

Would he be a good father to his child? How was a guy supposed to know *how* to be a daddy? Brenda would be a fantastic mother, he just knew that she would, but what caliber of father would he be?

Brenda. She was a very important part of his life and had been for over a year. During that year they'd both been dating, seeing people socially, with the hope of finding their soul mate, falling in love, making plans to marry and start a family. Both he and Brenda had zeroed out in that department...big-time.

Now Brenda was going to be the mother of his child. But she wouldn't be his wife, had refused his offer of marriage. She was probably right in having done that because, heaven knew, they were poles apart on everything from running an organized home with food in the refrigerator and clean clothes in the dresser drawers to the kind of music they liked.

As best friends none of that mattered, but as husband and wife? Man, talk about being incompatible. They'd probably last about five minutes if they attempted to live under the same roof.

So, he wasn't getting married. He wasn't head-over-heels in love. He hadn't found his soul mate among the masses. But he *was* going to be a father.

Richard sighed, dragged both hands down his face, then stared up into the darkness.

He was feeling a tad sorry for himself, a bit cheated that he wasn't going to have the whole package like the rest of the MacAllisters had. He was surrounded by happy marriages, couples who were so in love they couldn't see straight, family units made up of Mom, Dad and the cute little kids.

Even his brother, Jack, who had been a confirmed bachelor had popped up at the MacAllister family reunion last Christmas with a brand-new wife, son and another baby on the way. What a shocker that had been, and how obviously happy Jack and Jennifer were together. And Joey? What a nifty kid he was.

Was he jealous of his big brother? Green with envy when he envisioned the other couples in the MacAllister clan? Yep, he guessed he was, which wasn't a very flattering assessment of himself, but it was definitely and undeniably true.

"Well, get over it, MacAllister," he said, scowling into the darkness. "Count your blessings and shut the hell up...and go to sleep while you're at it."

Richard turned onto his stomach, then in the next instant rolled back over to where he had been.

He cared for Brenda very, very much, even loved her. But that love was based on a deep friendship, was not knock-your-socks-off romantic love like the other MacAllisters had together.

Richard's hand slid across the bed to where Brenda had lain when they'd made love. Now *that* had been a romantic night, no doubt about it. The lovemaking shared with Brenda was beyond belief in its intensity, had been...well, beautiful, really special, which was rather confusing whenever he allowed himself to dwell on it.

Ah, hell, forget it. That had been one night that was not going to be repeated and was best forgotten. Well, it couldn't exactly be completely erased, as it had resulted in The Newsflash.

And now here he was again, full circle, about to rake himself over the coals once more, wondering if he would be a decent father.

Richard yawned and closed his eyes.

So, okay, he thought sleepily, he wasn't going to have the whole rosy picture of wife, hearth and home. But he would stand by Brenda, be there for her and their baby through the good times and bad.

Yeah, he needed to count his blessings.

He was going to have a child to help raise to the very best of his ability.

And he already had a best friend, which was something a lot of people never had in their entire lives.

What was that weird thing Michael had yapped on about, regarding husbands, wives and best friends? Or was it best wives and friends, or—hell, he couldn't remember, and it hadn't made any sense at the time, anyway.

At last sleep won the battle warring in Richard's mind and he drifted off into a restless slumber.

Five

Brenda planted herself in front of the grocery cart and extended one hand, palm out, like a police officer stopping traffic.

"Halt, Richard," she said, laughing. "Don't you dare put another thing in this cart. Eating for two does *not* mean you buy two of everything." She shook her head as she was overcome by a fit of laughter.

Richard reached around Brenda and balanced two packages of frozen broccoli on top of the tower of food already in the cart.

"Don't be difficult," he said, smiling. "This is serious business. Your cupboards are bare, Mother Hubbard, and I'm not getting on that airplane tonight unless I know you and Flash will be eating properly while I'm slaving away in Tulsa."

"Me, Flash and what army?" Brenda said. "I don't need all this stuff. I probably don't even have enough room in my refrigerator and cupboards to put it."

"No problem. You have a key to my apartment. We'll store the overflow at my place if need be."

Brenda rolled her eyes heavenward.

Richard rested his hands on her shoulders. "I've hardly seen you all week since I brought you home from Kara and Andrew's wedding, Bren. I know this is a busy time at the travel agency, and you've been working long hours, and I have a sneaking suspicion that you have been snacking, not sitting down and consuming well-balanced meals. Correct?"

"I haven't been hungry," she said, frowning. "All-day morning sickness doesn't do much for a person's appetite, you know."

"Well, according to that material Kara gave you, the morning sickness should be over soon."

"I asked you to help me find where I put that packet in my apartment," Brenda said. "You didn't have to read all of it."

"Yes, I did," he said. "I want to know what's going on every step of the way. You and Flash are *not* alone, Bren. I want you to remember that."

"Ohhh, that's so sweet," Brenda said, sudden tears filling her eyes. She waved one hand in front of her face. "Stop, stop. This crying at the drop of a hat is so ridiculous."

"It's very endearing." Richard kissed her on the forehead. "Let's go check out, then I'll put everything away when we get back to your place while you rest. You aren't going to spend your day-off standing on your feet. You need to relax.''

"Quit being so nice to me," Brenda said, sniffling. "It will start the waterworks all over again."

"Go for it," Richard said, pushing the heavy cart down the aisle. "It's a natural part of the hormonal upheaval of pregnancy. It would probably be harmful to Flash if you attempted to suppress your emotions."

"You're weird, Richard," Brenda said, falling in step beside him. "I don't suppose you know how long you'll be in Tulsa?"

"Nope," Richard said, shaking his head. "Never can tell in advance about these assignments, but I'll call you every night while I'm away."

"Whatever for?"

"To check on how you are," he said. "I'll also ask you what you ate that day. Oh, and don't forget the schedule I taped to your refrigerator for drinking your milk. That is vitally important."

"Yes, master," Brenda said, glaring at him.

Richard chuckled and pushed the cart into line at a checkout counter.

Look at all that food, Brenda thought, staring at the grocery cart. She'd never had so much to choose from at one time since she'd been living on her own. She would have to hold herself back or she'd turned into a fat little piggy, which was what she was going to look like soon enough, thank you very much.

Brenda slid a glance at Richard, who was scanning the headlines of the variety of tabloids in the racks by the checkout line.

Richard was being so wonderful, she thought. So

thoughtful and caring. She felt very pampered and special, which was different from the norm. A person could get used to this.

No, she was getting carried away here. Richard was fussing over her because of Flash, not her. He was focused on the baby, his child, not the mother.

Richard used to make derogatory remarks about her unorganized kitchen, but he'd never hauled her to the grocery store to rectify the situation before. He was assuring himself that the baby would be properly nourished while he was away.

Brenda sighed.

She was feeling strange again, sort of blue and...and lonely. She didn't want Richard to go to Tulsa for heaven only knew how long. Granted, she'd hardly seen him in the week since they'd been at the wedding together, but she'd known he was there, just a whack on the wall away.

Brenda shook her head in self-disgust.

This was crazy. Richard traveled constantly, always had, always would. She was very accustomed to saying goodbye, then going about her own business until she heard his thumps on the wall announcing that he was once again home.

So why was she pouting—yes, pouting, for heaven's sake—because he was flying out tonight? It was probably her pregnant hormones overreacting again, which was getting very annoying.

"A two-headed dog?" Richard said, bringing Brenda from her gloomy thoughts. "How can people pay good money to buy those tabloids? Dumb." He looked at Brenda. "Which reminds me, now that we're talking about reading. I read an article the other day about reading to your unborn child. I don't suppose you own any of the classics, do you?''

"No," Brenda said, "and forget it. I'm not coming home from a long day at the travel agency and reading *War and Peace* out loud, for Pete's sake. Give me a break."

"Yeah, okay," Richard said thoughtfully, "we'll settle for listening to classical music. I'll bring over my CDs before I leave."

"You will not," Brenda said, planting her hands on her hips. "I hate that kind of music. It's either a waltz that lasts so long the people would pass out from exhaustion if they danced through the whole thing, or it's a military march number that would wear out even professional soldiers. I'm a country-western fan, Richard, and you know it."

Richard leaned down to speak close to Brenda's lips. "My child is not going to start life believing that happiness is a pickup truck, a bottle of beer and a willing woman, Bren."

Brenda burst into laughter. "This is the most insane conversation I've ever taken part in. There is no proof that listening to a certain kind of music, or reading specified material to an unborn child, makes one bit of difference to the baby."

"Oh, I don't know about that," the woman in line behind them said. "When I was pregnant with my first baby, my husband read the political section in the newspaper to my stomach every night. The kid was so upset he had colic for four months after he was born."

Brenda and Richard stared at the woman with wide eyes.

"I'm kidding," the woman said quickly. "I swear it, I'm just making that up. You two are so cute. You know, first-time parents-to-be, and I couldn't resist. Hey, just relax a bit and enjoy. I have four kids now, and they survive in spite of all the mistakes you make, and believe me, you'll make some beauts."

"Oh," Brenda said, frowning.

"Next?" the cashier said.

Richard pushed the cart forward and began to unload the groceries.

Mistakes? Brenda thought, plunking a can of orange juice on the moving mat. Had her parents made mistakes while raising her? If they had, she couldn't think of anything at the moment. Well, there was the time when she was four or five years old and had wanted a birthday cake shaped like a hippopotamus and they got her a dinosaur instead, but that hadn't warped her psyche for life.

Mistakes? Gracious, it was really sinking in that this motherhood role was tremendously complicated. What if she made a horrible mistake?

"Richard," she whispered.

"Mmm?" he said, busily emptying the cart.

"We don't know squat about babies," she said, still whispering. "What if we mess it up big-time? Don't you think this is a tad terrifying?"

"Why are you whispering?" Richard whispered.

"Because I don't want everyone in this store to know that I'm a potentially unfit mother."

"Don't stress, Bren," Richard said. "It's not good for Flash. We'll do all right. We'll read books, go to classes, conduct an in-depth survey among the MacAllister clan. Heaven knows, there are a slew of kids in my family and they're all neat little munch-kins.''

"Oh? And just when are we going to do all this?" Brenda said. "You're never home, remember? You travel more than you stay put."

"Did you say paper or plastic?" the cashier said.

"Paper," Brenda said.

"Plastic," Richard said at the same time.

"Is this a major decision in your lives, folks?" the cashier said.

"Half of the stuff goes in paper and half goes in plastic," Richard said.

"Whatever," the cashier said.

"Quit thinking," Richard said to Brenda. "You're getting all in a stew because you're tired."

"I am not tired!" Brenda said, then threw up her hands as she saw six people turn and look at her. "I give up. I need a nap."

"I rest my case," Richard said smugly. "Stick with me, Bren, I'm really getting the hang of this thing."

Oh, yes, Brenda thought with a weary sigh, she would definitely stick with Richard...like glue... until she got a better handle on what she was suddenly dealing with. After all, being there with emotional support during times of turmoil was what best friends were all about.

During the following weeks Brenda was extremely busy at the travel agency. At the end of each day she'd arrive home, exhausted. Despite her fatigue she waited eagerly for Richard's nightly telephone call and the long conversation they would share.

Richard had been away for two months when Brenda sat in Kara's office, waiting for her doctor and friend to appear. Kara had given her a quick once-over, then had been called to another examining room for an emergency.

The nurse had apologized for the interruption, then told Brenda to get dressed and make herself comfortable in Kara's office.

Brenda pressed one fingertip to her forehead in an attempt to push an imaginary button and turn off the Strauss waltz that was floating endlessly through her mind.

She'd decided a few weeks ago that since Richard was taking such a sincere interest in all aspects of her pregnancy the least she could do was cooperate. So, she'd scooped up some of his classical music CDs from his apartment and alternated her listening between them and her favorite country-western.

During one of Richard's nightly telephone calls he'd whooped in delight when he'd heard his familiar music playing in the background as he talked to her.

Such a little thing, Brenda thought, yet Richard had seemed so genuinely pleased that she had added his choice of music to her and Flash's leisure hours. He'd even admitted that he was hearing a lot of country-western music in Tulsa and it wasn't all pickup trucks, bottles of beer and willing women. There were some very nice songs, he'd acknowledged, about true and forever love.

They'd been exchanging some dynamite trivia over the telephone during the past weeks. Great stuff on both their parts, and she would guess they were about even on the scoreboard.

Richard had informed her that two-thirds of the world's eggplant was grown in New Jersey.

She had countered with the fact that there was no word in the English language that rhymed with silver, purple, month or orange.

Richard had come back with the statement that a cat had thirty-two muscles in each ear.

She had topped his cat with a goldfish, the poor little fishy having a memory span of only three seconds.

Richard had really outdone himself when he told her that a dime had 118 ridges around the edge.

"Such fun," Brenda said aloud as she smiled, then frowned in the next instant.

Fun, she thought. Yes, the ongoing trivia contest was a kick. It belonged to her and Richard, a special game they played only with each other. But there was so much more taking place during and after those nightly calls. Her heart quickened at the sound of Richard's greeting when she answered the telephone. And when he laughed or even chuckled, a strange little shiver would course through her at the rich, masculine sound.

Brenda sighed.

Every night when she replaced the receiver on the telephone she had to force herself to remove her hand, to sever the link with Richard.

Oh, dear heaven, she missed him so much. It was a new and frightening emotion because when he'd been gone for long stretches of time in the past, she'd hardly thought of him at all. Now? She wanted Richard here, with her, not hundreds of miles away.

What was happening to her? She thought frantically, pressing her hands to her cheeks. What did it all mean? If she was slowly but surely falling in love with Richard MacAllister, she'd never forgive herself. And she'd never be able to mend a heart shattered by loving a man who was not in love with her.

No, no, no, she was *not* falling in love with Richard.

Was she?

The door to the office opened and Kara rushed in, shaking her head as she sank into the chair behind her desk with a sigh.

"One of those days," she said, smiling at Brenda. "I'm sorry to have kept you waiting like this."

"No problem," Brenda said, relieved to be pulled from her troubling thoughts. "One of the perks of being the manager of Wishing Well Travel Agency is that I can juggle my schedule when the need arises."

"Nice," Kara said, nodding.

Brenda frowned. "Of course, I'm the one who has to solve all the glitches that come up, too. People often believe that if they nag at me long enough I'll miraculously find room on a cruise, or in a hotel, that is booked full. Oh, well, I really like my career, which is more than a lot of folks can say."

"That's very true," Kara said. "I love my chosen profession, too, but I certainly do cherish my roles of wife and mother, as well."

"How's baby Andy?" Brenda said.

"Growing like a weed," Kara said. "He's doing so well, and at this age, at least, there are no longer signs of any effects from the drugs his birth mother took. If something shows up in the future, Andrew and I will simply deal with it.'' She paused and looked at Brenda intently. ''It's marvelous to have a partner when you're raising a child, Bren. Have you told your baby's father that he's going to be one...a father?''

''Yes, I have,'' Brenda said, smoothing the material of her slacks over one knee and averting her eyes from Kara's. ''He immediately said that we should get married, but I nipped that in the bud.''

''Why?''

''We're too different,'' Brenda said, meeting Kara's gaze again. ''He's a neatnik, I'm a messy-Bessy at home. Our tastes are poles apart in music and... Well, I don't actually hate the Strauss waltzes now that I've really listened to some of them, but...

''He thinks a home should be run like...like I do the travel agency—organized, efficient, but I just wing it. He's into a regimented exercise routine, and I'm a couch potato.

''Besides, he's hardly ever home. He's thrilled about the baby, wants to be the best father he can be, but, gracious, he travels the majority of the time. Being married to him wouldn't change that, and could very well destroy our friendship, which is very important to me.

''He's being very attentive by long distance—he's in Tulsa at the moment—calls me every night to see how I'm doing and how Flash is. We call the baby Flash because my finding out I was pregnant was The Newsflash...with capital letters. Anyway, the subject of marriage has been dropped and...''

''Oh...my...goodness,'' Kara interrupted, sinking

back in her chair. "It's Richard. The father of your baby is my brother, Richard."

Brenda's eyes widened. "I never said that, Kara. Where on earth did you get such a...a crazy idea?"

"Strauss waltzes," Kara said, leaning forward again. "Neatnik. Organized. Tulsa. Traveling all the time. *Your friend.*"

"Oh." Brenda shifted uncomfortably in her chair. "I guess I was blithering on there a bit, wasn't I? Yes, well...Kara, did you know that an ostrich's eye is bigger than its brain? Just thought I'd whip a little trivia on you there."

"That's very fascinating information," Kara said, narrowing her eyes. "Has Richard gathered a lot of great trivia while he's been in Tulsa to share in the game you two have played forever?"

"Oh, yes, he is really on a roll and— Would you cut that out, Kara?" Brenda said. "That wasn't fair. Were you an FBI agent in a former life? You snuck up on me and— No, that wasn't fair at all."

"Am I correct in saying that Richard MacAllister is the father of your baby?" Kara said.

Brenda sighed. "Yes, he is. It just...just happened, that's all. It was one night...one...when we were both vulnerable, feeling sorry for ourselves because we can't seem to find our soul mate, the person we were meant to love, spend the remainder of our days with, and...we agreed, Richard and I, never to allow the...it...to be repeated. We would just forget it and continue being best friends."

"But you got pregnant that night."

Brenda nodded as she struggled against tears.

"And Richard is happy about the baby? Stepped right up and asked you to marry him?" Kara said.

"Yes, but I refused for all the reasons I've already opened my big mouth and listed," Brenda said, sniffling. "Richard and I would never survive together under the same roof. I need him to be my best friend, Kara. Can't you see that? I need to know he's there for me, no matter what, just as he's been for the last year and a half."

"But—"

"No, don't try to change my mind because you'd be wasting your breath," Brenda said. "Richard and I would be a complete disaster as husband and wife. Besides, I don't love him like that...romantically, I mean. I love him as my buddy, pal, my chum.

"I won't marry anyone who isn't my soul mate. I intend to love my husband with all my heart and know that he returns that depth of love in kind. To marry Richard because of the baby would be a terrible mistake, and it isn't going to happen."

"Okay," Kara said.

Brenda eyed her warily. "That's it? Just...okay? You're not going to deliver a twenty-minute speech on why I should marry your brother?"

"Nope," Kara said pleasantly. "You've obviously made up your mind on the subject, and that's that." She paused. "Now then, let's look at how you're doing here." She shifted her gaze to the file in front of her on the desk. "You said you're over your morning sickness, which is good."

"I'm eating everything in sight and stuff I don't even like is delicious," Brenda said. "Aren't you even going to say that it would be best to marry

Richard so that the baby has his name, is legally a MacAllister?''

"No, it's none of my business," Kara said. "Your blood pressure is fine, weight is fine. You're a generally fine mommy-to-be."

"I'm fat. I can't close the button at my waist on my slacks and skirts. Am I supposed to be this chubby this soon? And don't you want to point out that I should take what I can get, and that marrying my best friend is better than nothing, that I should just forget about the fairy-tale romance part?"

"No-o-o," Kara said slowly, "but I will say that I consider Andrew to be my best friend, as well as my soul mate."

"Oh, for heaven's sake," Brenda said, throwing up her hands, "you sound like Michael. He said something like that about Jenny, and neither Richard nor I understood what he meant. A best friend is in a totally different category from a romantic lover, a soul mate, Kara. It's like…like apples and oranges."

"Is it?" Kara said, raising her eyebrows.

"Yes, definitely," Brenda said. "See, the thing is, I don't believe that you or Michael have ever had a best friend…not like Richard and I are."

"Ah," Kara said.

"If you had," Brenda rushed on, "you'd understand what I mean when I say you can't compare that kind of relationship with a forever-love type." She nodded. "There. That explains it. You and Michael are speaking from a lack of experience."

"Ah," Kara said again.

"Yes, indeedy," Brenda said. "Richard and

I...being best friends, you realize...know of what we speak. End of story.''

''Ah.''

''Would you cut that out?'' Brenda said, frowning. ''You sound as though you're waiting for someone to stick a tongue depressor in your mouth to see if you have a sore throat or something.''

Kara laughed. ''I'm just letting you know that I'm listening to every word you're saying. Do note that I didn't conclude by announcing that I agree with you.''

''Whatever. Kara, do you think the MacAllister clan, all of the zillion of you, is going to accept The Newsflash and the fact that Richard and I never intend to marry? You're very conventional, family-oriented people and...well, I'd feel just terrible if this created a problem for Richard. Or for me, for that matter. I adore all of you.''

''Give us a little credit, Brenda. MacAllisters love unconditionally. No one will be passing judgment on you and Richard, and the baby will be welcomed with opened, loving arms.''

''Thank you.'' Brenda sighed. ''I guess when Richard calls me tonight I'll have to confess that I spilled the beans here today.''

''He phones *every* night from Tulsa?''

''Mmm,'' Brenda said, nodding. ''He's working seven days a week so he can get home as quickly as he can to check on me and Flash in person.''

''Which, of course, only a best friend—which I have no concept of—would do,'' Kara said, smothering a burst of laughter.

"Mmm." Brenda frowned. "Could we change the subject and discuss why I'm so fat so fast?"

"Every woman is different, Brenda. I've seen women who were still wearing their regular clothes the day they delivered a full-term baby. Others? Well, they pop, as the saying goes, very early. You don't have a big-boned frame—you're slender, delicate, and you're obviously going to show sooner rather than later."

"Dandy," Brenda said. "Wouldn't you know it? That means Richard and I will be facing the 'Why aren't you two getting married?' bit sooner rather than later, too. Ugh. Well, at least my parents are making no noises about returning anytime soon from Greece. That just leaves the MacAllister group to deal with." She rolled her eyes heavenward. "All million zillion of you."

"Don't worry about the family," Kara said, getting to her feet. "When you and Richard decide to make your announcement, you'll be pleasantly surprised by the reception you'll receive. I guarantee it. In the meantime your secret is safe with me."

"That's good to know," Brenda said, rising.

"Brenda," Kara said, "let me be certain that I understand where you're coming from. You believe that Michael and I are out in left field by saying that our soul mates are our best friends, due to the fact that we've never had a best friend separate and apart from our soul mates. Right?"

"Well, yes," Brenda said, nodding, "that sums it up quite nicely."

"It's sort of like you and Richard having the inside track on trivia," Kara went on, "because you've been concentrating on your game together for over a year. Correct?''

"Yes, that's a very good comparison. Experience is the best teacher, Kara.''

"Got it,'' Kara said, starting toward the door. "Make an appointment for a month from now before you leave.'' She opened the door and turned to look at Brenda. "Oh, and, Brenda? Did you know that Winston Churchill was born in a ladies' room during a dance his mother was attending? That, sweet Bren, is top-of-the-line trivia. Think about it.''

Brenda opened her mouth, shook her head slightly, then snapped her mouth closed again. Kara disappeared from view, leaving the door open behind her. Brenda walked slowly across the room, a frown on her face.

"What I think,'' she said aloud, "is that you set out to confuse me, Kara MacAllister Malone, and you did a super-duper job of it.''

Six

That night Brenda sat propped up against the pillows on the bed, the telephone receiver pressed to her ear as Richard ranted, raved and swore.

"The guy was a con artist, no doubt about it," Richard said. "He just threw this computer system into place, collected his money and split. The cops are looking for him, that's for damn sure, because this isn't the only company he took for a ride. What a mess. The lousy part is, I've finished fixing this disaster, but the schnook sold these good ol' boys *two* setups. One here in Tulsa and a link to their Dallas office. I'm flying to Texas in the morning to start all over again."

Brenda sat bolt upright on the bed, her hold on the receiver tightening.

"You're not coming home?" she said.

"No," Richard said, then sighed. "I was trying to figure out a way to make a quick trip to Ventura, but I just can't. The Dallas branch of this company is literally shut down without their computer system. I have to get over there right away."

"Oh," Brenda said, her shoulders slumping. "Well, yes, of course, that makes sense…I guess. No, cancel that. It definitely makes sense. It's just that I…"

Brenda's voice trailed off and she frowned.

She missed Richard, wanted him here, home, with her…right now. The strange part was that this was a different kind of *missing Richard* than she'd experienced in the past. A feeling she was growing more accustomed to.

She couldn't quite put her finger on what the difference was, but it was definitely there. It was causing a dark cloud of gloom to settle over her as it really sank in that Richard wasn't going to thunk on the wall to announce his arrival home for heaven only knew how long.

"It's just that you…what?" Richard said.

"Oh, well, nothing. I'm sorry you're having such problems, Richard."

"Me, too," he said. "The only bright spot in this picture is that I now know what's wrong with the system, and it shouldn't take me as long to fix the one in Dallas as it did here."

"How long?" she said quickly.

"I can't say for certain…maybe a month, instead of the two that I've spent here."

"Another whole month?" Brenda said, nearly shouting. She pressed her free hand to her forehead and flopped back against the pillows. "Ignore me, Richard. I sound like a nagging wife."

Richard chuckled. "If you'd marry me, you'd have the right to nag your little heart out, Bren."

"No, thank you." Brenda paused. "Do you need to vent some more about the crummy situation there? I'm not rushing you to wrap it up, I was just wondering if you were finished yet."

"Yeah, I'll shut up," he said. "Dumping it on you isn't going to change anything."

"I'm more than happy to listen."

"I know that, Bren, and I appreciate it. So! How are you? And how's Flash? Hey, wait a minute. You had an appointment with Kara today. Bring me up to date. What did she say?"

"I'm fine. Flash is fine," Brenda said. "But I'm fat, really Porky Piggy."

Richard laughed. "I seriously doubt that, Brenda. You're only three months pregnant."

"I kid you not, Richard. I can't button my slacks or skirts. Kara said that I'm apparently going to be one of those women who pop—that's the jargon— pop early. Everyone is going to know about Flash much sooner than I was thinking they would."

"Well—"

"Richard," Brenda interrupted, "I have to tell you this and I'm really, really sorry. I was chattering away, you know how I do sometimes, and I was dropping clues left and right without realizing that I was, and Kara…sort of…kind of…Richard, Kara figured out that you're the father of this baby."

Brenda took a much-needed deep breath, then re-

alized there was nothing but dead silence coming
from the telephone receiver.

"Oh, dear," Brenda said. "You're furious, aren't
you? Kara did promise that she wouldn't tell any of
your family that you...that we— I'm just so, so
sorry."

"Whoa," Richard said. "Slow down. I'm not an-
gry, Bren. Not at all. As far as I'm concerned the
entire MacAllister clan can be told about The Newsflash right now."

Brenda sat up again.

"Don't be absurd," she said, her eyes widening.
"There are going to be enough months of them asking why we aren't getting married and...no. No way.
No one is going to know until I can't camouflage my
condition anymore. Promise me that you won't tell
the MacAllisters yet, Richard. Please? Promise?"

"Okay, okay, don't stress, Bren. But when I come
home we need to have a serious discussion."

Brenda narrowed her eyes. "About what?"

"I'd rather wait until I see you, because this is
very important," he said quietly.

"Richard, that's not fair," Brenda said, her voice
rising again. "I'll sit here and stew. I'll go nuts trying to figure out what's on your mind. My brain will
be so preoccupied I'll probably forget to follow my
milk-drinking schedule."

"That's blackmail, Bren."

"Whatever works."

Richard swore under his breath, and Brenda
cringed.

"All right," he said finally, "you win, but I really
did want to sit you down, face-to-face, to talk about

this." He paused. "Brenda, in spite of the long hours I've put in here, I've still had a lot of time to think when I get back to the hotel at night. Lots of time."

"And?" she said tentatively.

"That is my baby you're carrying."

"No," Brenda said, "it's *our* baby."

"You know what I mean," he said. "I want *our* child to have my name, be a MacAllister. I need her to know that I'm proud and happy to be her father, never cause her to have one minute's doubt that I want her very, very much."

"Ohhh," Brenda said, her eyes pooling with tears. "That is so sweet."

"Just listen, okay?"

"Yes. Right." Brenda sniffled. "Sorry."

"I know you don't believe we should get married, Bren," Richard went on, "because we're such opposites and also because you feel that being in love, romantically in love, not best-friend love, is vitally important when those vows are taken."

"Yes."

"So, I don't know what the answer is here," he said. "I can't ask you to give our daughter my last name as though you didn't exist. The only solution, I guess, would be to hyphenate our names, have her be Baby Girl Henderson-MacAllister."

"That's an awful lot for a child to learn how to spell in first grade, Richard," Brenda said, frowning.

"I know, but it's really important to me that she have my name…somehow. Will you think about this while I'm gone, then we'll discuss it further when I get home?"

"Okay. Sure. I'll give it a great deal of thought."

Brenda paused. "Richard, why do you keep calling this baby a girl, referring to it as 'her'?"

Richard laughed. "Because she *is* a girl, Bren, guaranteed. I'm a MacAllister, remember? You know all about the Baby Bet that Forrest aced time after time.

"Then Ted Sharpe snapped Forrest's winning streak and since then the daddies have nailed it. Whatever the father says the baby is going to be is etched in stone.

"Jack's buddy, Brandon, over in Arizona, said he and his wife, Andrea, were going to have a girl and…bingo…they did. Now Jack has announced that he and Jennifer are having a boy…who is due in about a month, now that I think about it. Believe me, Jennifer will have a baby boy.

"Anyway, we're having a girl, Brenda. You can take that all the way to the pink booties bank."

Brenda splayed one hand gently on her slightly rounded stomach.

"A daughter," she said, awe ringing in her voice. "A precious little girl. You're making her seem so real, Richard."

"She is and she's ours, Bren," he said quietly. "She's our daughter, our miracle."

"Yes," Brenda whispered.

A strange warmth seemed to weave through the telephone lines to wrap around each of them, drawing them close, so close, in a special and meaningful moment.

Then slowly, but very surely, the soft warmth became pulsing heat that ignited desires and brought forth the sensual memories of the lovemaking they had shared so many, many weeks before.

"Bren, I…" Richard said finally, his voice husky. He stopped speaking and cleared his throat.

Brenda blinked, snapping herself back from the passion-laden place she'd floated to.

"Yes, well, I'd better let you get some sleep," Richard said. "I'll call you tomorrow night from Dallas. I'm really sorry that I'm going to be gone so long, Brenda. I wish I was there with you."

"I wish you were, too," she said, "but I understand why you can't be. You've always been gone a great deal and always will be, I guess. That's just the way things are because of your career."

"I've been thinking about that, too, but… Take good care of yourself and Flash. 'Bye, Brenda."

"Good night, Richard," she said quietly.

The dial tone buzzed in Brenda's ear. She replaced the receiver, then stared at it for a long moment.

"I miss you, Richard," she said, then drew a deep, wobbly breath that held the echo of tears. "I didn't even tell him about Winston Churchill."

Richard sat on the edge of the bed in his hotel room, his hand still on the telephone.

He didn't want to break the connection he had to Brenda, he realized, not releasing the receiver. He felt as though he'd been gone forever and was never going to get back to Ventura. To Brenda. And their daughter, who was nestled within Brenda's delicate body.

The nightly telephone calls just weren't cutting it, weren't enough. He wanted to see Brenda, give her a hug, reassure himself that she was all right. He wanted to place his hand on her stomach, her Porky Piggy stomach according to her, and bond through the palm of his hand with his baby girl.

Richard sighed, forced himself to pull his hand from the telephone, then stretched out on the bed, lacing his fingers beneath his head.

He wanted to go home. He didn't care if that sounded like a pouting kid who had been sent to camp. He wanted to go home...to Brenda.

He also wanted to marry Brenda Henderson, he thought dryly, to buy a house they'd make into a home, become a family...mom, dad and daughter.

But that wasn't going to happen, because Brenda would never agree to marry him, because they weren't *in* love with each other.

"Ah, hell," Richard said aloud, frowning as he stared up at the ceiling. "Everything is so damn complicated."

Why couldn't Brenda see that what they had together was special, that being best friends was important and meant a great deal, was more than some people ever had together?

So, okay, they weren't dewy-eyed, romantically in love with each other, but, hey, what they *did* have was rich and real and counted for something. They'd be a united front, a devoted set of parents to their daughter, and raise her in a home that was filled with sunshine and laughter.

Richard chuckled and shook his head.

A home that was a cluttered group of rooms that would include an empty refrigerator because Brenda couldn't find the notes she'd written to herself reminding her to pick her stuff up off the floor, then go for groceries.

Yeah, well, so what? He could be in charge of shopping for their food and he could afford to hire a service to keep the place in order. He could even live with country-western music as long as a few Strauss waltzes were played now and again.

Damn, why was Brenda being so difficult, so…so female, with her tough stand on being part of a fairy-tale love story?

Now that he really thought about it, how did a person even know when they were *romantically* in love? What ingredients had to be in the mix for that kind of love to take place? Did Brenda know? Did he? He didn't have a clue as to the answer to that one.

He was surrounded by MacAllister couples who were deeply in love with each other. What did they have together that he and Brenda didn't have as loving best friends? What would it take for Brenda and him to be best friends who were in love? He had no idea.

All he was certain of tonight, in this empty, sterile hotel room, was that he missed Brenda Henderson, wanted to see her smile and her sparkling dark eyes.

For the first time in all the years he'd been traveling with this damnable job, he was lonely.

He wanted to go home.

With another deep sigh, Richard swung his feet to the floor, tugged off his shoes, then headed for the shower, dreading another long night of tossing and turning…and yearning.

* * *

Brenda was extremely busy during the following three weeks as people scrambled to take one last trip out of the city before summer ended and school started. The telephones rang almost constantly at Wishing Well Travel Agency, and Brenda and her staff of three hardly had time to sip a hot cup of coffee or catch up on each other's news.

Brenda arrived home each evening so exhausted she had to tell herself to put one foot in front of the other as she entered her apartment. She ate dinner, took a soothing bubble bath and crawled into bed to await Richard's nightly call.

When it became obvious to Richard that he had wakened her from an early sleep three nights in a row, he lost control.

"Damn it, Bren," he said, "it's not even nine o'clock and you're so tired again you were sound asleep. It doesn't take a genius to realize that you're working too hard at the travel agency. This has got to stop. Are you listening to me, Brenda?"

Brenda yawned. "Mmm. I hear you, Richard. Things will calm down at the agency in a couple of weeks after Labor Day. It's always like this in August."

"Yeah, well, you haven't *always* been pregnant in August," he said gruffly. "Being totally exhausted night after night can't be good for you and the baby. Does Kara know you're pushing yourself like this?"

"I haven't spoken with Kara. I'm scheduled to see her next week. Quit yelling at me, Richard. I have responsibilities that go along with my career, just as you do. I'm not jumping on your case because you're working seven days a week, am I? No, I am not."

NO POSTAGE
NECESSARY
IF MAILED
IN THE
UNITED STATES

BUSINESS REPLY MAIL
FIRST-CLASS MAIL   PERMIT NO. 717   BUFFALO, NY

POSTAGE WILL BE PAID BY ADDRESSEE

SILHOUETTE READER SERVICE
3010 WALDEN AVE
PO BOX 1867
BUFFALO NY 14240-9952

Play The
Lucky Hearts Game

and get...
FREE BOOKS & a FREE GIFT...
YOURS to KEEP!

yes! I have scratched off the silver card.
Please send me my **2 FREE BOOKS**
and **FREE MYSTERY GIFT**. I understand
that I am under no obligation to purchase any
books as explained on the back of this card.

Scratch Here!
then look below to see
what your cards get you...

326 SDL C6KE   **225 SDL C6J9**

NAME   (PLEASE PRINT CLEARLY)

ADDRESS

APT.#   CITY

STATE/PROV.   ZIP/POSTAL CODE

Twenty-one gets you
2 FREE BOOKS and a
FREE MYSTERY GIFT!

Twenty gets you
2 FREE BOOKS!

Nineteen gets you
1 FREE BOOK!

TRY AGAIN!

Visit us online at
www.eHarlequin.com

DETACH AND MAIL CARD TODAY! (S-D-OS-10/00)

© 1998 HARLEQUIN ENTERPRISES LTD. ® and TM are
trademarks owned by Harlequin Books S.A., used under license.

"*I'm* not the one who's going to have a baby," he said, none too quietly. "What about your *responsibilities* to Flash?"

Brenda narrowed her eyes. "Don't you dare insinuate that I'm not taking proper care of our child, Richard MacAllister. I don't see you here pouring me glasses of milk. I'm doing this all alone and I'm not neglecting my health or the baby's. So just...just stop nagging me."

Richard sighed. "You're right. I'm not there with you, and I should be. I'm sorry I hollered at you, Bren. I feel as if I'm on another planet instead of being only a couple of states away from you." He paused. "You *are* drinking your milk, aren't you?"

"Aaak," Brenda yelled. "You're driving me crazy."

"Sorry, sorry, sorry," Richard said quickly. "We'll change the subject before you make plans to murder me. Want to hear some Texas trivia?"

"Sure," Brenda said, then yawned again.

"Okay, this one is right on the mark, considering the volume of some of this conversation we're having. Ready? The longest one-syllable word in the English language is screeched. How's that?"

"Not bad," Brenda said, nodding. "I just happen to have one in the language area myself. *Dreamt* is the only English word that ends in the letters *mt*."

"Really? I dreamt about you last night, Bren," Richard said quietly.

"You did?" she said, her voice hushed. "What was the dream about?"

"It was kind of a mishmash...you know how dreams can be, but the gist of it was that we were dancing…waltzing, I think, to Strauss in a big, crowded ballroom. You were wearing a long, flowing dress, and I had on a tux. Then suddenly we were dancing in a field of flowers.''

''Ohhh,'' Brenda said, ''how romantic. Waltzing in a field of flowers. Ohhh.''

''That's romantic?'' Richard said, frowning.

''I swear, Richard, I don't think you'd recognize romance if it bit you on the nose. What else happened in the dream?''

''It got nuts after that,'' he said. ''We were dancing, then…blam…we were holding babies. A whole bunch of babies, trying to juggle them in our arms because there were so many of them. Weird.''

''It's symbolic,'' Brenda said. ''We'll be juggling our careers and leisure time with caring for our baby. That's a rather daunting, even overwhelming, thought.''

''But not in the dream, Bren. We were laughing, having a wonderful time with the babies. It was fun. Then my alarm went off and woke me up. But the fact remains that we were thoroughly enjoying the dancing *and* the arrival of the munchkins.''

''Oh. Well, that's comforting,'' she said. ''Are you sure we were waltzing? Maybe we were doing the Texas two-step in time to country-western music.''

''It was *my* dream, Brenda. It was a Strauss waltz. Don't try to change the script.''

''Don't get grumpy again,'' Brenda said. ''I think it's very sweet that you dreamt about me and Flash. That there was a whole slew of babies in your dream is probably due to our baby being such a major player in our lives, necessitating all kinds of adjustments on our parts.''

"Since when did you become an expert on deciphering the meaning of dreams?"

"I'm just winging it here," Brenda said.

"Well, you're making sense," Richard said. "Things will be easier for both of us when I get home. Then you won't be alone and I won't feel so…so left out of what is happening.''

"But you'll leave again in a few days…a week at the most, Richard. You always do.''

"We'll see. I'm going to hang up so you can go back to sleep. Maybe I'll dream about you again tonight.''

"That would be nice," Brenda said softly.

"Or maybe you'll dream about me.''

"Yes, maybe I will," she said. "That would be nice, too.''

"Good night, Brenda.''

"Good night, Richard. Have…have sweet dreams.''

Three nights later Brenda dashed into her apartment and grabbed up the receiver to the ringing telephone.

"'Lo," she said, gasping for breath.

"Brenda? This is Jillian MacAllister.''

"Hi, Jillian," Brenda said. "How are you? And Forrest? And the triplets?''

"We're all dandy. Listen, you're on my list for the MacAllister-family calling tree. Jennifer is in labor at Mercy Hospital even as we speak.''

"Oh, what exciting news, Jillian," Brenda said.

"And how lovely it is to know that I'm on the MacAllister-calling tree list."

"Well, you're like a member of the clan, Bren. Anyway, some of us are going to the hospital, and others are staying home with the kiddies. I'm here on triple-bubble-bath-and-bed duty, but Forrest left already for the hospital. He said that Jack was coming unglued when he called. If Jack faints in the delivery room, he'll never live it down."

"That's for sure," Brenda said, laughing. "Poor Jack. I hope he hangs in there. Jillian, just think, Jennifer and Jack's son is going to be born on this very night."

"Ah, I see that you're a believer in the Baby Bet. Jack said they are having a boy, so it's a boy."

And this, Brenda thought, splaying one hand on her tummy, is a girl, because Richard said so.

"I'm going to go to the hospital right now, Jillian," she said. "Thanks so much for calling me."

"My thoughts and prayers will be at that hospital," Jillian said, "even if I can't be there in person. 'Bye, Bren."

"'Bye."

Brenda hung up the receiver, grabbed her purse and hurried to the door. She rushed forward as soon as she flung it open and proceeded to slam into an immovable object, causing her to yelp in surprise. She looked up, and her eyes widened.

"Richard!" she said. "Richard?"

"In the flesh," he said, smiling as he wrapped his arms around her. "Ah, man, it's great to see you, Bren."

Brenda nestled her head on Richard's chest, savoring the solid warmth of him, inhaling his familiar aroma, drinking in the feel of his strong arms encircling her as she wrapped her arms around his back.

"I'm glad to see you, too," she said, tilting her head back to meet his gaze. "Why didn't you tell me you were coming home?"

"I wasn't positive that I could finish up in Dallas," he said, "but I did, and I'm here, and where were you going in such an all-fired hurry?"

"Oh! To the hospital. Jennifer is in labor. Jillian just telephoned me, because I'm on the MacAllister family calling tree. Isn't that special? I was so touched.

"Forrest said that Jack is falling apart. Forrest will probably get a bet going as to whether or not Jack will pass out in the delivery room.

"Do you think your brother will be able to stay on his feet long enough to see his son born? It *is* a boy, you know, because Jack said it's a boy, just like you said that we're having a girl and—"

Richard kissed her.

He kissed Brenda because he was so very glad to see her at long last and because he was so relieved that he was actually home.

He kissed her because she looked like a delicate summer flower in her pretty dress and because her dark eyes were sparkling like rare diamonds with the excitement of the pending birth of Jennifer and Jack's son.

He kissed her because she was carrying *his* daughter, and that fact still caused him to be filled with awe at the very thought.

He kissed her because she was Brenda, and he'd missed her very, very much.

He ended the kiss with a reluctance that was rather unsettling, then saw a matching emotion of confusion on Brenda's face.

"You're home," Brenda said breathlessly. Well, duh, that was a less-than-brilliant thing to say, she thought, but it was a wonder she could even speak at all after that kiss. That wonderful, breath-stealing, passionate kiss that she'd returned with total abandon. Oh, mercy, what was happening here? "Richard?"

"I'm...I'm just glad to be back," he said, his voice slightly gritty. "I didn't plan to kiss you like that, but I...I did. So, sue me, or slug me, or—" Richard stopped speaking and his eyes widened as he stared at Brenda, who was still nestled to him. "Oh, Bren, I can feel our baby pressing against me. Your stomach is..."

"Porky Piggy," she said, laughing. "See? I told you I was getting fat fast."

Richard gripped her shoulders and eased her away from him, his gaze shifting to Brenda's stomach, which was covered by the blousy top of her dress. He raised one hand, then hesitated and looked directly into her eyes.

"Is it all right if I— What I mean is, I'd really like to— But if you don't want me to..."

Brenda took Richard's hand and placed it on the gently rounded slope of her tummy, her hand covering his.

"Richard," she said, smiling at him warmly, "this is your...our daughter."

"Hey, Flash," he said, "how's it going in there? This is me, your father, your daddy. I'm home, baby girl."

But for how long? Brenda thought, a shiver coursing through her. The very image in her mind of Richard once again packing his suitcase and leaving her all alone was so depressing, so bleak and empty. She didn't want him to leave her, not again.

Why? she asked herself in the next instant. So he'd be available to kiss the socks off her at every turn? She didn't want to sue him or slug him, she wanted him to kiss her again and again and again.

Oh, this was insane. And this train of thought was going to stop...right now. This was Richard, her best friend, who just happened to be the father of the baby she was carrying.

The kiss they'd just shared didn't mean anything in the overall picture. Richard had just gotten carried away by the moment, by the joy of being home, by the awe and wonder of his child. He hadn't kissed *her,* he'd reacted to their *situation,* the *circumstances* surrounding it. And she'd responded to that kiss for the same reasons.

There. She'd figured it all out. Thank goodness. Everything was fine, under control, hunky-dory. Except for the fact that she was standing in the open doorway to her apartment with Richard MacAllister's hand splayed on her stomach, for Pete's sake.

"Are you coming to the hospital with me to wait for the arrival of your new nephew?" Brenda said, removing Richard's hand from her stomach.

"What?" Richard shook his head slightly. "Oh, yes, you bet. I wouldn't miss it. But are you certain you should go? You've no doubt had another long, hard day at the travel agency.''

"I'm fine," Brenda said. "Let's hit the road. I just hope that everyone is so busy concentrating on Jennifer and Jack that they don't take a long look at me in this dress. A practiced eye, which the MacAllisters have, would see in a second that I'm pregnant. We've been so busy at work that no one has noticed yet. I'm just not ready for your family to know about this baby, Richard.''

Well, he was more than ready, Richard thought, as Brenda closed the apartment door. He wanted to tell the entire MacAllister clan—hell, he wanted to announce to the world—that he was going to be a father, that he and Brenda were going to have a baby.

Richard encircled Brenda's shoulders with one arm as they started down the hallway.

And even more, he thought, he wanted to marry Brenda Henderson. Living next door to her wasn't going to cut it for him. No, sir. He wanted to be part of his child's life every moment that it was humanly possible.

Somehow—but how?—he had to convince Brenda that they didn't have to be in love with each other in order to be husband and wife, that being best friends was enough, was an honest and steady foundation on which to base their future, and one that would allow them to raise their child together.

As Richard drove toward the hospital he glanced over at Brenda.

"Trivia," he said, redirecting his attention to the traffic. "The dragonfly has a lifespan of twenty-four hours.''

"Really?" Brenda said. "That's rather sad, isn't it?" She laughed. "Don't tell me things like that, Richard. My pregnant hormones will probably cause me to weep for a week about the poor little dragonflies."

"Well, it makes a person think," Richard said, sliding a quick look at her. "We humans are blessed with years and years of living, and we owe it to ourselves to reach out and grab hold of whatever happiness is in front of us. It may not be picture perfect, the way we fantasized or daydreamed about, but, by golly, some is better than none."

"I wonder what Jennifer and Jack are going to name their son," Brenda said.

Richard's shoulders slumped and he frowned.

So much for being profound and meaningful. He'd struck out big-time with that one, that was for damn sure.

But he now had a mission, a purpose, a goal. He was a MacAllister, and MacAllisters fought the good fight and won. He would marry Brenda Henderson. She'd see the light, come to view things as he did, realize that while, no, they weren't *in* love with each other, they did love and respect each other.

They were best friends.

They would be a family—mother, father and daughter.

They would raise their child and rejoice in the wonder of the miracle they had created together.

And they would never, ever again…be lonely.

Now all Richard needed was a plan to make it all come true.

Seven

The waiting room on the maternity floor at Mercy Hospital was crowded with MacAllisters when Brenda and Richard arrived.

Both sets of senior MacAllisters were there, as well as representatives from each of the families except for Ryan and Deedee, and Ted and Hannah, as the police officers of the group were on duty and the mommies were home with the children.

Forrest did, indeed, have a bet going as to whether or not his cousin Jack would pass out in the delivery room. The betting was very detailed with money being placed on Jack surviving the ordeal on his feet or fainting dead away before, during or after the arrival of his and Jennifer's son. That Jennifer would have a boy was a given in everyone's mind.

"Thank you, thank you," Forrest said to Richard,

as he smacked a twenty-dollar bill into Forrest's hand. "You're late so you get the dregs. About all I've got left is Jack hitting the deck in his own kitchen when he gets home. You want it?"

"That will do it," Richard said, nodding. "He'll be cool here under pressure, then lose it later."

"Got it," Forrest said, scribbling on a piece of paper. "Hey, remember, Richard, I've got twenty on you in the Bachelor Bet. Just keep on keeping on in your swinging single lifestyle, cousin. You've always been a confirmed bachelor, and if you change your mind, I'm going to pop you a good one."

"I fully intend to maintain my present way of thinking," Richard said.

Which was that he wanted a wife, children and a real home, he mused. He always had, but he hadn't been about to let this group know he couldn't seem to find his soul mate among the multitudes. Forrest would really pop him in the chops if he knew that his so-called "swinging single" cousin Richard fully intended to marry Brenda Henderson...somehow.

"Glad to hear it," Forrest said. "I sure wish someone would figure out how long you and that Sheriff Montana over in Arizona have to stay single before I can collect some money on you guys. This is a sloppy bet, this bachelor thing. That's because I didn't set it up."

Brenda laughed. "You're so full of yourself, Forrest MacAllister. There's certainly nothing wrong with your self-esteem."

"Hey, what can I say?" Forrest said, grinning. "If you've got it—hey."

"Gag me with a spoon," Michael said from where

he was slouched on a sofa. "Don't talk to him, Brenda. He's a waste. Say, does anyone know what Jack and Jennifer are going to name this baby?"

"Nope," Ralph MacAllister said. "Jack said they'd know for sure when they saw the baby. I already have a namesake thanks to Kara and Andrew in the form of Andrew Ralph MacAllister Malone, so…" The grandfather-to-be shrugged. "I don't have any idea what they'll name him."

"Hopefully we won't have to wait too long to find out," Mary MacAllister said, reaching over to grasp Ralph's hand. "This waiting is wicked."

"You get used to it after a half a dozen or so grandchildren, Mary," Robert MacAllister said. "Isn't that right, Margaret?"

"No," his wife said, laughing. "No matter how many times you sit in this room, you feel helpless and the time just drags by." Margaret paused. "Brenda, come sit by me, dear. I haven't seen you in so long."

Brenda crossed the room to settle onto a sofa next to Margaret MacAllister. The buzz of conversation picked up again, the subject now being the current winding down of the professional baseball season.

Margaret MacAllister smiled warmly at Brenda, then squeezed one of Brenda's hands.

"I wanted you to sit here with me out of view, Brenda, dear," Margaret said quietly. "The way you were standing, just so, made it very easy to tell that you're expecting a baby.

"I wasn't certain you wished that to be publicly known, since you haven't said anything about it. If I'm wrong, then you just jump right back up and make your announcement while you have at least this many MacAllisters gathered.''

The color drained from Brenda's face, and she attempted, and failed, to suck in her stomach.

''Oh, dear heaven, no,'' she whispered, ''I don't want to make an announcement about...'' She looked quickly around the noisy room. ''Do you think anyone else— Oh, this is terrible, just awful.''

''Hush, hush,'' Margaret said, patting Brenda's knee. ''Don't upset yourself. You're like a member of this family, Brenda. No one is going to censure you. If you're happy about your baby, then we'll be just as thrilled for you. MacAllisters put great stock in happiness. *Are* you pleased about your child?''

Brenda produced a small smile. ''Yes...most of the time. When I'm really exhausted, I often get scared to death, but...'' She nodded. ''I love this baby already, and I want her very much.''

''Good. Perfect,'' Margaret said, smiling. ''That's what matters. You know it's a girl? You've had an ultrasound done?''

''Oh, um, no. No, I didn't have an ultrasound,'' Brenda said, mentally scrambling for something to explain her slip of the tongue. ''Maybe it's a boy. Boys are nice. Yep, they're cute little things, those baby boys. Then again, it could be a girl. Then again...''

''Hi, Aunt Margaret,'' Richard said, suddenly appearing in front of the pair.

''Hello, Richard,'' Margaret said, smiling up at him. ''How delightful that you could be here for your brother's big event. I thought you were in Texas.''

''Just got home tonight.'' Richard hunkered down

in front of Brenda and splayed his hands on her knees. "I've got a buck that says you didn't have any dinner, Bren. How about I go down to the cafeteria and get you a sandwich and a glass of milk and bring it back up here?"

Brenda slid a near-panicky glance at Margaret, then looked at Richard.

"No, thank you, buddy Richard," she said, staring at him intently, "I'll eat something when I get home. You just go talk to your cousins and do your guy thing. Goodbye, Richard, *my pal.*"

Richard frowned. "You've got dark smudges beneath your eyes, Bren. I didn't notice them before we came. If this drags on too late here, I'm taking you home so you can get some rest."

"Richard," Brenda said through clenched teeth, "go away. I'm sure that everyone would love to hear all about Dallas. Go say something to your family in Texan…or whatever."

"Maybe one of the vending machines on this floor has those little cartons of milk," Richard said.

"Oh, good grief," Brenda said, dropping her face into her hands.

Richard shifted his hands to his thighs and pushed himself to his feet.

"That's the ticket," he said. "I'll go check out the vending machines."

Brenda kept her hands in front of her face and raised her head enough to peer through her fingers to be certain that Richard was gone. She peeked at Margaret MacAllister, then nearly groaned aloud when she saw Richard's aunt narrow her eyes, then smile and nod.

Brenda dropped her hands from her face and clutched them tightly in her lap.

"So!" she said brightly. "Is Joey excited about having a new baby brother? I assume he's with Jillian or Hannah or...Joey is so cute. Just adorable. He'll be a super big brother, don't you think, Margaret? Sure. Hasn't it been humid lately. August is just so soggy, you know what I mean? I—"

"Richard will be a wonderful father," Margaret said. "All the MacAllister men are devoted daddies. I take it that Richard has decreed that you're having a girl? Then you are, because that's how the Baby Bet goes now. The daddy knows without a doubt. I'm thrilled for you both, Brenda, I truly am."

"Oh, but...Richard who?" Brenda said, batting her eyelashes.

Margaret laughed. "All right, I won't say any more about it. You and Richard love each other, are expecting a baby and beyond that your plans are none of my business. I'm sure you'll inform the family about your news when you're ready, and that's just fine."

"Margaret, listen to me," Brenda whispered. "Richard is my best friend and I'm his best friend. Yes, we love each other, but not...not romantically, not *in* love, just best-friend love. We're not getting married because that *in* love just isn't there."

"My dear child," Margaret said, "I sat in this very room thirty-one years ago and awaited the birth of Richard MacAllister. I know and love that boy as much as I do my own sons.

"You should also remember that Richard has the expressive MacAllister eyes. I just saw him speaking

with you, looking at you. Oh, yes, Brenda, our Richard is most definitely *in* love, no matter what you
might think to the contrary. That's not to say that
he's *aware* of the depth of his emotions for you yet,
but—''

"No, no, no," Brenda said. "I don't mean to
sound disrespectful, Margaret, but you're very
wrong. Richard and I are best friends...nothing
more. This—" she waved her hand in the direction
of her stomach "—just sort of...happened. I re-
peat—Richard and I are best friends, buddies, pals.
End of story."

"Mmm," Margaret said. "The thing is, Brenda,
that my darling Robert is my best friend, too, as well
as my soul mate."

"Your family has a weird take on that subject,"
Brenda said, frowning. "Really off the wall."

"Hey," Richard said from across the room, "look
who I found clad in fashionable surgical greens.
Ladies and gentlemen, may I present my brother,
Jack, the newest daddy of the clan. Oh, and here's
my baby sister, Kara, straight from the delivery
room, too."

Everyone got to their feet and started talking at
once. Brenda drew a steadying breath, then joined
the group.

Jack raised his hands for silence.

"I did *not* pass out," Jack said. "Not before, during, nor after the birth of Jennifer's and my son, nor
will I conk out later, in case that got into the betting
pool."

A wide grin broke across Jack's face.

"It's a boy, of course," he went on, "because I

said it was, and he weighs seven pounds, seven ounces. Jennifer was fantastic, and the baby is yelling his head off. I—'' Emotions choked off his words for a moment. ''I am truly blessed.''

''What's his name, son?'' Ralph said.

''His name is Jason,'' Jack said, then shifted his gaze to Richard. ''Joey and Jason. It has a nice rhythm. Yep, he's Jason…*Richard*…MacAllister.''

Richard's eyes widened, then got suspiciously bright and glistening.

''You…you named your son after me?'' he said, his voice husky. ''Ah, man, Jack, I don't know what to say. That's— I mean…thank you.'' He glanced around quickly. ''Hey, Bren, where are you? Did you hear this? Jennifer and Jack named the baby Jason *Richard* MacAllister.''

Brenda moved to Richard's side, and he encircled her shoulders with his arm and pulled her close.

''Isn't that something?'' Richard said.

''That's definitely something,'' she said, smiling.

All eyes were trained on the pair as they continued to smile at each other.

''Well,'' Margaret said, stepping quickly in front of Brenda and Richard, ''when can we see Jason Richard? Jack? Kara?''

''I'll go check,'' Kara said. ''In the meantime, give this new daddy a hug, family. He did just great. No visitors for Jennifer tonight except for Jack, but Jason Richard will be on display in the nursery. I'll be back in a second.''

Hugs, handshakes and slaps on the back were exchanged, and the buzz of chatter started up again.

When Richard released Brenda to give Jack a bear hug, Margaret stepped close to Brenda.

"Richard is definitely *in* love," Margaret whispered. "Now you must determine how *you* feel about him, during the time you have while he's discovering the truth of his emotions regarding you."

"But..." Brenda said.

"Don't rush it, dear," Margaret said. "Time holds all the answers."

"But..."

"Jason Richard MacAllister," Kara said from the doorway, "is now ready to receive his guests."

"But..." Brenda said again, raising one finger as Margaret walked away, "you're wrong and..." She sighed. "Never mind."

"Come on, Bren," Richard said. "Let's go see my namesake."

Jason Richard MacAllister was beautiful, Brenda mused, when it was her turn to step close to the nursery window and see the baby. So perfect. He had fuzzy strawberry-blond hair and rosy cheeks and, oh, he was adorable. But, good gracious, he was tiny. She'd never really paid attention before to just how small newborn babies were.

"What do you think?" Richard said, moving next to Brenda. "Neat kid, huh?"

"Yes, he's fantastic," Brenda said, "but he's so tiny, Richard, and helpless and... How does a person hold a child that small without smushing him?"

"Very carefully, I guess," he said, chuckling. "I don't know, Bren. Natural instincts kick in and you just do it." He shrugged. "Can't be all that tough.

Even Forrest managed to help tend to the triplets when they were little without breaking them.''

"I heard that, Richard," Forrest said. "I'll have you know that I was a pro within a week of the girls coming home from the hospital. Hey, there must be some kind of bet I can get going on the proficiency of new daddies. Hmm. I'll think about that.''

"Say good-night to Jason Richard, everyone," Kara said. "Visiting hours are over. Jack, go kiss your wife good-night. I'm off for home to share this news with Andrew. 'Bye for now, family.''

Goodbyes and congratulations were expressed to Jack, then the group went down in the elevator and separated in the parking lot, everyone heading for their vehicles.

Brenda was quiet during the drive home as she replayed over and over in her mind what Margaret MacAllister had said to her.

Margaret was a wonderful and wise woman, Brenda thought, but this time Margaret was wrong. Richard MacAllister was not *in* love with her.

And she certainly wasn't *in* love with him, either.

It had just been wishful thinking on Margaret's part. She simply wanted her nephew to have what all the other MacAllister couples did. But it just wasn't there, that romantic love that Margaret was so certain she had observed in Richard's expressive Mac-Allister eyes.

Brenda sighed, then frowned as she heard the strange sadness echoing in her own sigh.

That was silly. Facts were facts. It was nothing to get gloomy about. She and Richard just weren't *in* love with each other. They were best friends who loved each other in that best-friend way, and that was that.

Brenda sighed again, then told herself crossly to knock it off.

"What's wrong, Bren?" Richard said, glancing over at her. "You sound sad or something."

"No, no, I'm just tired," she said quickly. "And hungry. And thirsty. Need some milk. I'm going to get home, eat, drink and go to bed."

"Sounds like a plan," Richard said, nodding. "You need your nourishment, your milk and your rest." He paused. "Jason *Richard* MacAllister. What a special gift Jennifer and Jack have bestowed on me."

"Yes, it's very special."

"Second only to the gift you're giving me, Brenda," Richard said quietly. "My daughter. *Our* daughter. The next time the MacAllister family gathers in that waiting room at Mercy Hospital it will be to await the arrival of *our* baby. That's a pretty awesome thought, isn't it?"

"It's awesome, all right," Brenda said, frowning, "and your aunt Margaret already knows that it's going to happen. She took one look at me and knew I was pregnant.

"Then, because you were going on and on like a motor mouth about my having something to eat and needing some milk and...well, Margaret figured out that you're the father in this charming scenario. How's that for awesome, MacAllister?"

Richard laughed. "No kidding? Aunt Margaret nailed it, huh? Well, it's next to impossible to get anything past Aunt Margaret. She's sharp as a tack. What a hoot."

"A hoot!" Brenda yelled, causing Richard to cringe in surprise at her outburst. "I'd call it a disaster, that's what I'd call it. I'm not ready for your family to know about this baby, Richard.

"I'm not even prepared to tell my *own* parents that I'm pregnant because I...I just don't know what to say, how to explain that I..." She sniffled. "This whole situation is not...is not a hoot, Mr. Mac-Allister."

"Gosh, Bren, I'm sorry," Richard said. "I didn't mean to upset you, I really didn't. Hey, look, we're almost home. There's just a couple of blocks left to go. I'll fix you something good to eat. Okay? Would you like your milk warmed? That's supposed to be a very soothing drink, warm milk. Yeah, that's what I'll do. I'll heat it up for you and—"

"Richard, stop being so nice to me," Brenda said, throwing up her hands. "I just screeched at you like a shrew and—"

"Screeched," Richard said, "is, as we trivia experts know, the longest one-syllable word in the English language. Right?"

Brenda laughed and shook her head. "You're so crazy. It's impossible to stay upset at you. I'm sorry I was witchy."

Richard pulled into a parking spot and turned off the ignition.

"I'll speak to Aunt Margaret, Bren, and ask her not to tell anyone about the baby yet. Would that make you feel better?"

"No, it's all right. I'm getting fat fast, remember?

Everyone is going to know soon, so—" Brenda shrugged "—just be prepared to answer the zillion questions from your family about why we aren't getting married. Oh, ugh, I dread that part so much."

"I'll think of something to say," he said, opening the car door. Like…*Brenda and I are getting married next week,* or *Brenda and I were married* last *week,* or… Yeah, right. All he had to do was figure out how to convince Brenda to marry him. Whew. "I'll come around and get your door, Bren. Stay put."

"Why? You've never tended to my door before."

"Things are different now," he said, turning to look at her intently. "*Very* different."

Brenda frowned as she watched Richard cross in front of the vehicle.

He wasn't opening the door for *her,* she reminded herself. He was doing it for the baby. She just happened to be the one who was toting Flash around. And she had to be very careful to remember that.

Inside her apartment Brenda went to change into her comforting pea-soup robe, while Richard busied himself in the kitchen making omelettes and toast, which was his only choice, due to the lack of supplies in her refrigerator and cupboards.

They ate the meal in near silence, each lost in their own thoughts. Richard straightened the kitchen, then strode across the living room to the front door.

"I'll let you get to bed," he said.

"Oh, well, I feel much better now that I've eaten," Brenda said. "You don't have to leave yet."

"I have to unpack, sort my mail, the whole bit," he said. "I'll see you tomorrow. 'Bye."

And with that Richard was gone, leaving Brenda standing in the middle of the living room staring at the door he'd closed behind him.

"Well," she said. "Okay. Fine. I guess."

She walked slowly in the direction of her bedroom, then halted when a triple knock thudded on the door. She hurried to answer the summons, flinging open the door. Richard moved past her in a rush.

"Richard, what..." Brenda started.

He turned and looked at her with wide eyes.

"Ants," he said, not quite meeting her gaze. "My apartment has been invaded by ants. The little beggars are everywhere. They must have been hiding when I first got home before we went to the hospital, but their convention has been called to order now, by golly. Big-time. I'll have to sleep here...with you."

"What!" Brenda said, volume on high.

"On the sofa," he said quickly, then shivered. "Man, I can't stay over there with those creepy-crawlies."

"Go buy a can of ant spray and zap them," Brenda said, frowning. "You're bigger than they are, Richard."

"There are too many of them, Bren. The situation calls for a professional exterminator. I'll contact the landlord in the morning. For now I'll just borrow a pillow and blanket from you and crash on your sofa. No problem. I'll get the bed linens out of your cupboard, because I know where they are and you probably don't remember. Just pretend I'm not here. Go to bed. Good night, Brenda.''

Brenda opened her mouth, then snapped it closed again in the next instant when she realized she didn't have a clue what to say.

"Good night, Richard," she said, then made a hasty exit from the living room.

Richard watched Brenda go, and when she had disappeared from view he punched one fist in the air.

Yes! he thought. He'd done it. What a brilliant plan this was, and he'd pulled it off. He and Brenda were now living under the same roof.

The imaginary army of ants he'd invented was going to prove to be a hearty bunch, a new and strange species and immune to the usual chemicals that should be able to wipe them out.

Now he was in a position to prove to Brenda that while, no, they weren't romantically in love, they were still good together, that being best friends counted for a lot, would make it possible for them to marry and to raise their child in a real home with a mother and father.

His plan was in motion.

The battle had begun.

He had every intention of winning, and he would. He just had to.

Eight

"Trivia time," Brenda said to Richard.

"Lay it on me," Richard said, smiling.

They were seated at Brenda's kitchen table, consuming a delicious dinner that Richard had prepared while Brenda was at work at the travel agency. It was an old-fashioned meal of pot roast, mashed potatoes, gravy and cooked carrots. Brenda was enjoying every bite.

"Okay, here goes," Brenda said. "The national anthem of Greece has 158 verses, and there is no record of anyone ever memorizing all of them."

Richard laughed. "I know that, because I read the postcard you got from your folks today, and your mom had written it on the card. You don't get any points for that one, Bren."

"You read my mail, Richard?" she said, stiffening in her chair.

"No, not really," he said, lifting one shoulder in a shrug. "There's an unwritten law that says that postcards are public domain."

"There is no such law," she said with a little sniff. "Mail is mail. It's private."

"Wrong," Richard said, shaking his head. "Ask the postman who delivers the stuff. He'll tell you that postcards are open to public scrutiny. That fact is probably worth a few trivia points, now that I think about it, especially since you didn't know it was true."

Brenda laughed. "You cheat."

"I do not," he said indignantly.

"Yes, you do," she said, "but I'll forgive you because you had this fantastic dinner waiting for me when I came home. It's really yummy, Richard, and I appreciate it." She paused. "So, what's the word on your ants?"

"Nothing. I left two messages for the landlord but he hasn't returned my calls yet. I gave him my telephone number and yours, and both answering machines were on when I went to the grocery store, but...I'll start over again tomorrow trying to track him down."

"Oh."

"You don't mind my bunking on your sofa, do you, Bren?" Richard said. "I mean, if you're uncomfortable with it, I can always go to a hotel or sack out at my folks' place. My mom would be in seventh heaven if I was under her roof so she could tell me to get a haircut."

"No, no, I have no problem with your staying here," Brenda said. Except for the fact that she'd had a terrible time getting to sleep last night due to the fact that she was just so *aware* that Richard was sleeping in the next room. "Hey, I'm not totally nuts. I came home to dinner on the table, my cupboards and refrigerator full of goodies and my apartment cleaned from top to bottom. You're a handy roommate to have around."

He was going to stab himself in the heart with his fork, Richard thought dismally. Now he had the title of Brenda's roommate? Cripe. No, he mustn't get discouraged. He had just begun to fight.

"I had some free time, that's all," he said. "What I did was no big deal. I enjoy cooking and—"

"You can't stand clutter," Brenda said, smiling. "You picked up the mess in here because it was driving you crazy."

"Well, sort of. You know, Bren, if you would just put things back where they belong after you use them, you wouldn't lose things all the time," he said. "For example, you kicked off your shoes when you came home tonight. I can see one of them in the middle of the living room, but do you know where the other one is?"

Brenda shifted in her chair to sweep her gaze over the living room.

"Nope, can't see it," she said, then looked at Richard again. "It must be there somewhere."

"It's under the sofa."

"It is? No kidding? Well, I would have found it eventually."

"Yes, but think about it," Richard said, leaning

slightly toward her. "If you had taken a few extra minutes to go into your bedroom and put those shoes in the closet, they'd be ready for you to wear the next time you wanted them. It's very simple really."

"I'll give that theory a try...one of these days," Brenda said. "Oh, I don't know, Richard. I run the travel agency like a well-oiled machine, but when I get home I just want to...to..."

"Be a slob," he said, laughing.

"That's not nice," she said, unable to curb her own laughter. "I'm not sloppy at home, I'm...relaxed. There. That's good."

"Mmm," Richard said, cocking an eyebrow at her. "Project your kind of relaxation to when the baby is here. You've got to have plenty of formula prepared, can't run out of diapers in the middle of the night, have to keep the laundry up-to-date and on it goes."

Brenda frowned. "You've got a point there. Maybe I should start working on bringing my organizational skills home with me from the agency. I'll do that...maybe...later, in a few months. No, you're right. I should get my sloppy act together now. I'll have enough to deal with once the baby arrives."

"There you go," Richard said, beaming. "You'll really like having an efficiently run home, Bren. I guarantee that you will."

"Well, don't expect miracles," she said. "I can't change overnight, you know."

"But you *can* change if you put your mind to it," Richard said, suddenly serious. "We all can. Change. Our actions and attitudes aren't etched in stone. In order to grow as a person, we all need to be open to new ideas, be willing to adjust our outlooks and…and stuff.''

"Oh, okay," Brenda said, smiling. "I'll get right on it. I'll put my shoes in the closet every time I come home from work."

Richard frowned. "That's a start…I guess." He paused. "Would you like some cherry cobbler? I made it from scratch."

Brenda's eyes widened. "I'm too full for dessert now, but you made cherry cobbler from scratch? Who taught you to do that?"

"My dad," he said. "While we were growing up, Jack, my dad and I cooked dinner two nights a week and my mom did the other days. After Kara came to live with us, she was on my mom's team. Jack moaned and groaned his way through the cooking lessons, but I really enjoyed them."

"Amazing," Brenda said. "Why didn't I know about this before?"

"It didn't come up, I guess. Now it has because we're living together."

"Could you phrase that a bit differently, Richard? We're not *living together* we're just…" Brenda frowned. "Give me a minute here."

"We're living together," Richard said decisively. "We eat, sleep, hang out, under the same roof. That, in my opinion, is living together."

"Yes, but when you use the term *living together,* it indicates that the two people are having…are engaging in— What I mean is…" Brenda lifted her chin. "We're not sleeping together."

"That's true," Richard said thoughtfully. "Of

course we could make love if we wanted to.'' He shrugged. "Which we don't.''

"We don't?'' Brenda said, frowning.

"Of course not,'' Richard said, looking at Brenda intently. "The one night of lovemaking we shared was a fluke, the end result of a long list of circumstances that resulted in—'' He cleared his throat. "The truth of the matter is, Brenda, it resulted in the most incredibly beautiful lovemaking I've ever shared with anyone in my entire life.''

"Oh, I know,'' Brenda said dreamily, staring into space. "You'll get no argument from me on that one, Richard. It was so—'' she blinked "—forget it.''

"I can't,'' he said, covering one of her hands with his on the top of the table. "I've tried, believe me, but I just can't erase the memories of our night together from my mind. Plus the fact that it resulted in little Flash, there, makes it even more difficult to dismiss. It definitely happened, Brenda, and it was...was very special.''

"Yes,'' she said softly. "Yes, it was.''

The heat from Richard's hand was rushing up her arm and across her breasts like a wild current. Oh, gracious, now it was traveling throughout her, settling low and hot in her body.

Why, why, why was Richard having this kind of sensual impact on her? He was her best friend, not her lover. Well, he *had* been her lover for that one glorious night but... This was so unsettling and confusing. Enough was enough.

Brenda pulled her hand from beneath Richard's and got to her feet.

"You cooked, I'll clean the kitchen," she said. "That's only fair."

"No way," Richard said. "You worked all day, Bren. All I did was stop by my office and turn in my expense records. You go put your feet up, and I'll tend to this mess."

"You also shopped for groceries, cleaned the apartment and prepared a splendid meal." Brenda shook her head. "No, I'm straightening up the kitchen."

Richard stood. "We'll compromise, okay? We'll do it together."

"Well, yes, all right," she said, nodding. "It will get done twice as fast that way. Then I'm going to put on my pea-soup and watch *Casablanca* on television. Don't think I'm wearing the pea-soup because I'm upset or don't feel well. I wear it sometimes just because it's comfy."

"You were wearing your pea-soup the night we—" Richard cleared his throat and picked up their plates from the table. "I'm not sure I'll ever be able to see you in that awful robe again without remembering the— Never mind."

"Maybe I'd better not wear it while you're...while we're..."

"Living together," he said, taking the plates to the sink. "Lightning isn't going to strike you if you say it, Brenda. We're living together."

"Okay, fine," Brenda said. "So we're...we're living together. But only until you evict the ants."

"The what?" Richard said. "Oh! Yes! The ants. Yes, indeed, they should at least help pay the rent if they're going to live in my apartment.'' He started loading the dishwasher.

Brenda brought more dishes from the table and set them on the counter.

"Don't you think it's strange that the ants invaded only your place?" she said. "I haven't seen even one of those little guys over here."

"Who knows what goes on in the mind of an ant," Richard said. "Hey, there's a baseball game on the tube tonight that should be a great one to watch."

"But *Casablanca* is on," Brenda said.

"Bren, you've seen that movie at least twenty times," Richard said as he placed the dinner leftovers in the refrigerator.

"Twenty-two, but I never get tired of it," she said. "It's a classic, one of the most romantic films that was ever made."

"Mmm," Richard said, as he wiped off the counter, then rinsed the dishcloth. He turned and looked at Brenda. "All done. Kitchen is clean."

"Oh, so it is," she said. "I certainly didn't do much to help."

"Don't worry about it," he said. "Look, why don't I go to my apartment and lug my television over here. I'll watch the ball game with the sound off, and you can weep your way through your movie. How's that?"

Brenda smiled. "You're a genius."

"No, I'm just a man who is attempting to get a handle on compromising when living with a woman."

"And you're doing an admirable job of it,"

Brenda said, then stood on tiptoe to kiss Richard on the cheek.

He turned his head at that exact moment, and their lips brushed lightly as their eyes met. Time stopped. Hearts began to race in wild rhythms.

They each took one step forward to close the distance between them, Brenda's arms floating upward to encircle Richard's neck, his arms wrapping around her.

He captured her lips in a kiss that was searing, hungry, urgent, and Brenda returned it with total abandon, savoring the taste of Richard, the feel of his strong arms holding her fast, the heated sensations thrumming throughout her.

His arousal was heavy against her, and she rejoiced in knowing he wanted her as she did him. They were in a hazy, sensual place that was weaving a web around them…tighter, hotter, refusing to release them from its grip.

A groan rumbled in Richard's chest. A whimper caught in Brenda's throat.

Brenda Henderson, her mind hammered. What on earth are you doing?

She broke the kiss, drew a wobbly breath, then stepped backward, forcing Richard to release his hold on her.

"That…" she said, then took another breath. "That shouldn't have happened."

"Why not?" Richard said, his voice gritty. "Why not, Brenda? We want each other. There's nothing wrong with that."

"Nothing wrong?" she said, planting her hands on her hips. "My gosh, Richard, it's as tacky as it gets. We're talking about lust here. Sex. Not love-making between two people who love each other, just earthy, physically satisfying sex.''

"No," he said, shaking his head. "It's more than that. We're not strangers who just met in a singles' bar and decided to go for it. We respect each other, know each other better than some people do in an entire lifetime. We love each other, too, in our own way. We're best friends, Brenda, and that counts for something, it truly does.''

"It's not enough," she said, her eyes filling with sudden tears.

"Yes, it is," he said, gripping her shoulders. "Can't you see that, Bren? Being best friends is a solid foundation to base a marriage on. We can make it work if we put our minds to it, agree that's what we want to do. We'll be a family. You, me and our daughter. It'll be good, Bren. It will.''

"No, no, no," she said, dashing tears from her cheeks. "I see myself sitting on the foot of our daughter's bed when she's a teenager and she's day-dreaming about the man she'll marry someday.

"'Tell me about when you and Daddy fell in love,' she'll say to me. 'Tell me how romantic it was, Mom, how it felt, what your heart knew, then your mind. How did you really know, Mom, that Dad was your soul mate for eternity?'

"What would I say to her, Richard?" A sob caught in Brenda's throat. "'Well, kiddo, it wasn't quite like that. Your father and I are lusty best friends, that's all. Soul mates? No. *In* love with each other? Nope, never got that far. We're buddies, pals. We're—'''

"Stop it, Brenda, just stop," Richard said, narrowing his eyes as he dropped his hands from her shoulders. "That's enough."

"No, it's not," she said, wrapping her hands around her elbows. "Why are you willing to settle for less than what you've dreamed you'd have with a woman, Richard? You've been searching for your soul mate, hoping to find her, to have it all, just like the other MacAllisters do.

"Just because we've created a child together doesn't mean... Oh, Richard, don't you see? We're not in love with each other the way we should be to plan a life together as husband and wife." She sniffled. "We're just not...not *in* love."

"How do you know that?" he said, his voice rising. "Just what in the hell makes you such an all-fired expert on the subject, Bren?

"My family is harping on the fact that their soul mates are their best friends. How do you know that you and I, best friends that we are, aren't each other's soul mates? Did you ever stop to think that we could be *in* love and not even know it?"

Brenda lifted her chin. "Don't be ridiculous. We'd *know* it, if it was true."

"Oh, really? Well, spell it out for me. What are the signs, the signals, the feelings, the emotions, the...whatever...that a person has when they're *in* love? Come on, lay it on me."

"Well, how should I know?" she said, matching his volume. "I've never been *in* love in my entire life. I...I assume that...that a person can just tell when...just feels it...just knows...just—" She threw up her hands. "I don't have a clue as to how two people realize they're in love with each other. I really don't.''

Richard sighed. "I don't, either. What I believe is that what we *do* have together is enough to base a marriage on and raise a child.''

"No.'' Brenda shook her head. "No, it isn't.''

"Okay,'' Richard said, raising both hands in a gesture of peace. "The subject is closed…for now. I'll go get my television. Be a *buddy* and serve me a dish of cherry cobbler, would you? Thanks, *pal*.''

Richard strode past Brenda and headed for the apartment door.

"You don't have be so grumpy about it,'' she yelled after him.

"I feel like being grumpy,'' he said, yanking open the door. "So, damn it, I will.''

Brenda jerked as Richard slammed the door, then of their own volition her fingers floated upward to rest on her lips, which still tingled slightly from the intensity of the kiss she'd shared with Richard. She shifted her hands to splay them on her stomach.

"Oh, baby girl,'' she said, fresh tears filling her eyes, "I'm getting so confused, so muddled. Your mommy is a wreck, sweetheart. I just hope I can figure out my complicated feelings, because my relationship with your daddy—my entire future—is what's at stake.''

Nine

Brenda smiled as she entered her apartment, then frowned as she closed the door behind her, not having received Richard's cheerful greeting upon her arrival home from the travel agency.

"Richard?" she called, but was answered with only silence.

As she crossed the living room, walked down the hall and entered the bedroom, she was aware and rather unsettled by the fact that she was very disappointed that Richard wasn't home as he had been every evening for the past week.

She placed her shoes in the closet, changed into a pair of maternity slacks and a long T-shirt, then hung the loose-fitting dress she'd worn to work on a hanger.

Neat and tidy, she thought, laughing softly. She

was really getting the hang of this organization-at-home program, and it really hadn't been that difficult to do. All it had taken was for Richard to point out that she simply needed to apply the same skills at home that she used at the travel agency.

Where on earth was Richard? she thought, wandering back into the living room. A note. Maybe he'd left her a note, telling her where he was off to and when he'd return home.

A search of the kitchen, where no wonderfully aromatic dinner was cooking, revealed no clue as to where Richard was.

Brenda sank onto the sofa with a sigh, leaned her head on the top and stared at the ceiling.

This was silly, she admonished herself. She had no cause to feel so empty, so...so strangely lonely, just because Richard hadn't been at the apartment to welcome her home after a long day at work.

They'd only been *living together,* to quote the man, for a week, but she now realized how much she'd been enjoying Richard's company, and how very nice it was to have someone to come home to, to talk and share with over dinner and through the hours of the evening.

Darn it, she missed Richard and wanted him to walk through the door right this minute.

Get a grip, Brenda, she thought, clicking her tongue in self-disgust. This *living together* was a temporary arrangement. She knew that.

Richard was only going to be sleeping on her sofa until the army of ants in his apartment succumbed to the exterminator's chemicals—which Richard said gave him a terrible headache—or until he left on his next assignment.

She knew all that, accepted it. She just hadn't been prepared to come home to an empty apartment today. She'd bought Richard a present and had been looking forward to giving it to him at dinner.

How was it possible, she mused, that a lifestyle only one week old could seem as though it had been the norm for a very long time? She sure didn't know the answer to *that* question.

There had been no more kisses shared with Richard during the past week, nor had he brought up the subject again of their getting married. They'd simply lived their lives…so, okay, *together*…and it had been nice…so, okay, more than nice…and she really, *really* didn't like sitting here all alone and…so, okay, that was unreasonable but—

"Oh, hush," Brenda said aloud. "You're driving yourself crazy again, Brenda Henderson. You think too much."

The sound of Richard's key in the lock brought Brenda to her feet. She turned as Richard entered the apartment and kicked the door closed behind him, his arms filled with paper bags.

"Hi," Brenda said, smiling. "I was wondering where you were. Not that you're accountable to me, or anything like that, but I looked for a note, not that you're obligated to tell me where you are every second, but…I'm glad you're home, Richard."

Richard stopped in his tracks and looked at Brenda intently.

"Thank you," he said, smiling at her warmly.

"That's really nice to hear, Bren. It's good to be here, to be…be home."

There was half a room separating them as they smiled at each other. They didn't move, didn't need to close the distance between them, because they felt connected somehow, as though they were only inches apart.

Then their smiles disappeared as a feeling began to weave around them, creating a nearly crackling aura of sensuality, of heat, of pulsing desire that caused hearts to race and breaths to catch.

"Yes, well," Richard said finally, breaking the eerie spell and averting his eyes from Brenda's. "Yes. I didn't think I'd be gone so long, Bren, or I would have left you a note. That would have been the thoughtful thing to do, and I would have if I'd known that quitting my job was going to take so much time. I stopped and picked up Chinese food for dinner. I hope that's all right. I know you like Chinese so—"

"Halt," Brenda said, raising one hand as her eyes widened. "You quit your job? Your job? You quit? You did?"

"I did," Richard said, nodding. "Come on, let's eat while this stuff is still hot."

Brenda poured soda into tall glasses while Richard pulled small white boxes from the paper bags. He placed another small bag on the end of the table. Brenda put glasses, plates and forks on the table, slid onto her chair, then looked at Richard.

"I can't stand it another minute," she said. "You quit your job? Why?"

"Fill your plate," Richard said. "Flash is hungry. Where's your milk?"

"Milk would be yucky with Chinese food. I'll drink some later," she said, scooping food onto her plate. She took a bite and nodded. "Delicious. You quit your job?"

Richard raised one finger, consumed some food, then met Brenda's gaze.

"I went to see my boss," he said, "and told him that from now on I only wanted assignments that were close enough to be able to come home every night. He said that was absolutely impossible.

"So, I made a pitch for traveling where if I hadn't whipped the problem in two weeks, I would be replaced by someone else to finish it. He said that wasn't efficient nor feasible." Richard shrugged. "So I quit," he said, peering into a white box. "Want some rice?"

"I already have rice," Brenda said. "Richard, you've lost me here. I still don't understand why you quit your job."

"Bren," he said, leaning back in his chair, "I nearly went crazy while I was on that last assignment. All I could think about was that you were here alone, pregnant with my baby, and I wasn't with you. I want to be here every step till our child is born, not hear over the telephone that you're turning into Porky Piggy."

"Oh, thanks a lot." Brenda laughed, but quickly became serious. "That's very sweet, Richard, but don't you think that quitting your job was a rather drastic step?"

"Nope," he said. "Because I fully intend to stand by your side through the remaining months until our baby is born. And then? What kind of father could I

be if I was never home? I'd probably have to intro-
duce myself to my own daughter every time I came
back from an assignment, or wear a name tag or
something.''

"Now that," Brenda said, laughing, "was funny."

Richard leaned forward. "No, Brenda, there is
nothing funny about it. I am going to be a father and
that is very important to me. I want to be the best I
can be in that role and I can't accomplish that if I'm
hundreds, or even thousands, of miles away for
weeks at a stretch. Understand?''

Brenda nodded slowly. "Yes. Yes, I do, and I really respect and admire what you're saying. But
aren't you a little young to retire?''

"I'm not planning on sitting on my tush or hitting
a little white ball around a golf course every day. I'm
going to start my own company of computer troubleshooters," he said. "I'll personally take on the jobs
that are close by, and my crew will handle the traveling assignments.

"I have a great deal of money saved, because I
was on the go so much I really didn't have time to
spend it. My nest egg will see me through the lean
months that go along with starting a new company.

"I'll offer not only troubleshooting for systems
that are down, but also provide a service of analyz-
ing, recommending and installing computer packages
that will meet the needs of a client's firm. There.
That's it in a nutshell. What do you think?''

"I think…" Brenda started, then stopped speaking
as unexpected tears filled her eyes. "I think that our
daughter is going to be a lucky little girl to have you

for a father, Richard. I think you're…you're wonderful for putting her first and—'' She sniffled and shook her head.

"You're first, too, and so am I,'' he said. "What I mean is, you deserve better than to handle this pregnancy all alone while I'm off to hell and back. You shouldn't have to take care of the baby all alone, either, while I'm gone. You're just as important as Flash, Bren.

"The thing is, so am I. My needs are being met by this decision, too. I want, and will have, the opportunity to see you every day, watch you grow bigger with our baby, be there when she's born, then take part in every step of her life. I did this…quit my job…for all of us, for our…our family, which is you, me and baby girl MacAllister.''

"Ohhh,'' Brenda said. "Ohhh.''

"Oops,'' Richard said. "Here we go again.'' He reached into his back pocket for a clean white handkerchief and gave it to Brenda. "It's a good thing my folks always include a package of these among my gifts at Christmas. I have a big supply.''

"That number is dwindling,'' Brenda said, dabbing at her nose. "The washing machines consider your handkerchiefs a gourmet delight. Whoosh. They're gone.''

"That's something else I've been meaning to speak to you about,'' Richard said.

"What? That I should buy you a zillion new handkerchiefs?''

"No,'' he said, chuckling. "There are plenty left in my dresser drawer. I'm talking about not wanting you to do the laundry anymore. That's manual labor,

Bren, and you shouldn't be doing it. I'll tend to the wash from now on. If I don't have time to use the gobbling machines here in the building, I'll send it out to be done. The point is, you're not to worry about it."

"Ohhh," Brenda said, then smacked the handkerchief against her nose again.

"I'm waiting for you to react to the fact that I called our daughter baby girl MacAllister," Richard said. "I asked you to think about her having my name, remember? We haven't discussed it since I got home from Dallas. Did you? Think about it?"

"Yes, I did," Brenda said, nodding, "but I didn't see a solution. If the baby is a MacAllister and you're a MacAllister, I'd feel... Oh, I don't know, Richard...sort of like odd man out or something."

Not if you married me and became a MacAllister, too, Richard mentally yelled. No, don't do it. He had to keep his big mouth shut on the subject, not push Brenda about marrying him, or she was liable to toss him out on his ear and send him home to his apartment that was supposedly reeking with imaginary chemicals that were going to demolish the imaginary ants.

No, pleading his case about marriage had gotten him nothing more than daggers flashing from Brenda's gorgeous eyes and a stubborn, negative lift of her chin.

His best bet was to continue on as they were...living together, making it work as they co-existed each day and night, eventually cause Brenda to realize that what they had together was enough to base a future on.

But, oh, man, those nights were pure agony. Not only was Brenda's sofa lumpy as hell, but he kept having sensuous dreams about her when he did manage to sleep.

It was taking all the willpower he possessed not to march down that hallway in the middle of the night, slip into bed with Bren and kiss her senseless. Then they'd make such fantastically beautiful love together and—

"Richard?"

"What!" he said, much too loudly.

"Why are you yelling?" Brenda said. "Gracious."

"Sorry. My mind went off somewhere," he said. It trekked right into bed with you, sweet Brenda. "Where were we?"

"Baby Girl MacAllister," she said.

"Oh, yeah. Well, all right, we'll put that on hold for now because we don't have a solution at this point in time. How's that?"

"Fine. Oh, I bought you a present today, Richard. I saw it and thought of you and…I'll be right back."

Brenda hurried from the room and returned with a bag that she gave to Richard. She sat down again and smiled at him.

"Open it," she said.

Richard reached into the bag and pulled out a hardcover book.

"I'll be damned," he said, smiling. "I have here a book titled *So You're Going to Be a Daddy*. Thank you very much, Brenda. I'll read every word. You thought of me when you saw it?"

"Well, yes."

"Interesting," he said, reaching for the package he'd set on the end of the table. "This is for you. I saw it and thought of *you*."

Brenda pulled out the book that was inside the bag, and a gasp escaped from her lips.

"Oh, my goodness," she said. "You bought me *So You're Going to Be a Mommy*." She wrapped her arms around the book and hugged it to her breasts. "Is this weird, Richard? That we chose the same book for each other? Well, except for the mommy daddy thing. Don't you think it's rather…spooky?"

"I'm not sure," Richard said slowly, staring at his book. "Wait a minute." He looked at Brenda again. "Jack and I were chatting once, and he was telling me about his buddy Brandon over in Prescott, Arizona. Brandon had shared a story with Jack about his relationship with Andrea, the woman he married. They had a baby girl in the spring, remember?"

"Oh, yes," Brenda said. "Brandon was eligible for the MacAllister Baby Bet because he is such a close friend of Jack's. Brandon said early on that he and Andrea would have a girl and they did, of course. What does that have to do with these books?"

"Well, according to what Brandon told Jack and Jack told me, Brandon and Andrea had all kinds of problems to solve before they made their lifelong commitment.

"Anyway, they were together on a Christmas and lo and behold they gave each other the same gift. One of those small globe things that makes snow fall when you turn it upside down."

"They had no idea what the other person was going to give them?"

"Nope," Richard said. "Brandon has these terrific great-aunts—Aunt Prudence and Aunt Charity. Jack said they are nifty ladies. The aunts explained, on that Christmas, that the matching gifts meant that Andrea and Brandon were…were in love with each other, that it was a given, done, etched in stone. That's what it meant, Bren, the message of those matching gifts. Brandon and Andrea were…soul mates."

Brenda plunked her book quickly on the table as though it had suddenly become too hot to handle, then stared at it with wide eyes, her heart racing.

"That's…that's a romantic story," she said, her voice not quite steady. She met Richard's frowning gaze, matching his expression. "But it's just that— a story."

"It was true," Richard said quietly. "Brandon and Andrea are very happily married now and have started their family. It was true, Bren."

Brenda gripped the edge of the table and leaned toward Richard. "It has nothing to do with *us,* Richard," she said. "We know exactly where we stand emotionally in each other's lives. We're best friends. This book we bought each other is a…a coincidence, that's all."

"Brenda, come on, give me a break. There were a couple of hundred books on parenting to choose from in that store I was in, and I'm sure that's true of where you shopped." Richard waved his book in the air. "This means something, and I think we should address it. According to Aunt Prudence and Aunt Charity, you and I are—"

"No," Brenda said, smacking the table with the

palm of one hand. "You love me, Richard, but
you're not *in* love with me, no matter what your aunt
Margaret believes. All the time and attention, the
hovering around me, isn't directed toward me, it's
for the baby I'm carrying. I know that. You know
that. People who are *in* love are aware of that fact,
for heaven's sake."

"My aunt Margaret is convinced that I'm *in* love
with you?"

"Well, yes, and I tried to tell her she was wrong,"
Brenda said, waving one hand dismissively in the air.
"She said she could see it in your ever-famous
MacAllister eyes, or whatever, and she wouldn't lis-
ten to me when I—forget it. You are not *in* love with
me."

"Oh?" Richard said, raising his eyebrows. "Just
how does one know when one is *in* love? Hmm? Tell
me that, so wise and worldly Brenda."

"I'm not having this conversation, again, Richard," she said, then took a bite of her dinner.

"Why not?"

Brenda shook her head and kept chewing.

"You said that you know that I'm not *in* love with
you," Richard went on. "I didn't hear you say that
you're positive that you're not *in* love with *me*."

Brenda swallowed, then pointed her fork at Richard.

"Semantics," she said. "I meant that *we* know
that we're not *in* love with each other. The end.
Change the subject. Eat your dinner. Go check the
body count of ants in your apartment. I have enough
to deal with, Richard, without your muddling my
brain any further."

"But, Bren—"

"No." Brenda dropped her fork onto her plate, got to her feet and stepped backward, wrapping her hands around her elbows. "I'm going to have a baby, Richard, and sometimes I get so scared because I don't know if I'll be a proper mother, even though I want to be so very much.

"And today I wrote a long letter to my parents and told them that I'm pregnant, and somewhere in my heart I know they'll be supportive, but there's a niggling little voice in my mind that is so afraid they'll be disappointed in me because I'm not married and—"

"Brenda," Richard said, getting to his feet.

"Stay over there and just listen to me."

"Yes." Richard raised both hands. "Okay. I won't move."

"Thank you." Brenda drew a wobbly breath. "I get so tired sometimes, Richard, just weepy exhausted, and when I think about the future, trying to be a mother and continuing to excel at my chosen career and—

"Oh, yes, my career. I told the crew at work today that I'm pregnant, and they were all smiles and congratulations, but I could see unasked questions on their faces about who the father is and why aren't I marrying him and—

"It would be so much easier to just tell myself that I'm *in* love with you, and we'd get married and buy a house, and you'd be there to help all the time, and I wouldn't be so alone and terrified and…"

"Ah, Bren," Richard said, dragging one hand through his hair.

"There are times, Richard, when I'm afraid of myself." Brenda splayed one hand on her breasts. "Of me. What if I did it? What if I convinced myself that I'm *in* love with you and somehow found a way to…to brainwash you into thinking that you're *in* love with me, when we know we're not because we're just best friends? What then, Richard? What if I did that horrible thing just because I was so worn-out and…I'd ruin our lives, our daughter's life and… You and I would be together under false pretenses.

"Oh, it might be just fine and dandy for years, while our daughter was growing up and we were focused on her. But she'd eventually leave home to find her own path, which is the natural order of things.

"What then? You and I would look at each other and wonder what on earth we were doing there, sitting across the kitchen table staring at each other. We'd come to resent each other, because we'd have nothing left to go forward with."

Tears spilled onto Brenda's pale cheeks. "We'd have nothing left, and I would have lost my best friend in the bargain."

Brenda covered her face with her hands and gave way to her tears.

Richard closed the distance between them and wrapped his arms around Brenda, holding her close. He buried his face in Brenda's silky hair for a long moment, then raised his head again and sighed as Brenda struggled to stop the flow of tears that seemed endless.

"You're right, Brenda," Richard said, his voice flat and low. "The piper would eventually have to be paid, wouldn't it, if we attempted to base a marriage on just friendship. I really thought that we would be just fine if we— But I was wrong, I can see that now.

"Ah, hell, it wouldn't work. We're not *in* love with each other, and because we're not, it isn't enough. Aunt Margaret misread whatever she thought she saw in my damnable MacAllister eyes, and it was just a fluke that we bought each other the matching books and…and there are no ants."

Brenda raised her head, sniffled and frowned in confusion.

"What about the ants?" she said.

"I made it all up, Bren," he said, still holding her close to him. "I truly believed that if I could show you that we could live under the same roof, *live together,* that you'd come to realize it was enough to base a marriage on—our being best friends who had learned to compromise on our differences."

"You lied about the ants?" she said, her tear-filled eyes widening. "There isn't an army of ants in your apartment?"

"No," he said, his shoulders slumping. "I saw a ladybug on the leaf of one of my plants, but…no, there aren't any ants.

"I'm sorry I lied to you, Brenda, and I hope you'll forgive me for doing it, but I really believed that I was on the right track and— But I wasn't. I was very, very wrong. Friendship just isn't enough to have a…to have a forever."

"No, it's not," Brenda said, hardly above a whisper. "And, yes, I forgive you for the ant lie. It was actually very sweet of you, Richard, because you had to sleep on my crummy sofa to accomplish what you thought was best for us and our daughter.''

She managed to produce a small smile. ''Your plan wasn't a total loss,'' she said. ''I hang up my clothes and put my shoes in the closet every day now, and I haven't lost a list of what I'm supposed to do.

''I enjoy baseball, now that I know the rules of the game, and you yelled 'Stella' at the top of your lungs right along with Marlon Brando when we watched that movie together.

''We waltzed around the living room to Strauss and practiced the two-step to country-western music, and I've never run out of milk, and I'm going to miss you when I go to sleep at night and know you're not here and…and I feel so sad that I want to crawl into my pea-soup and cry for a week without stopping.''

Richard framed Brenda's face in his hands. ''Ah, Bren,'' he said, shaking his head. ''Why does everything have to be so complicated for us?''

Brenda sighed. ''I don't know, Richard, but it is, it just is.''

''Yeah.''

He kissed her on the forehead, then started to drop his hands from her face. Brenda gripped his wrists to keep his hands in place and looked directly into his eyes.

''Make love with me, Richard. Please?'' she said. ''We had one night together and in my mind it belongs to our baby because that was when we created her. I want memories of our lovemaking that are mine, all mine…and yours if you want them. Am I asking too much of you?''

"Ah, no, Bren, no, you're not." Richard brushed his lips over hers. "Flash had her night. This one is ours, yours and mine."

Richard's mouth melted over Brenda's, and a last, lingering sob caught in her throat. Heartbeats skittered, then settled into a rapid tempo, and the heat of desire rushed through them like a wild current.

Richard broke the kiss and lifted Brenda into his arms. He carried her to the bedroom, set her on her feet, snapped on the small lamp on the nightstand and flung back the blankets on the bed.

A sense of urgency suffused them. They were existing for now, in time stolen out of reality, creating a world that wasn't theirs to keep, nor to linger in.

They shed their clothes quickly and moved onto the bed, Richard catching his weight on one forearm as he splayed his hand on the rounded slope of Brenda's stomach.

"Are you sure we won't hurt her?" he said, his voice gritty with passion.

"She'll be fine," Brenda said. "This is *our* night, Richard."

"Yes."

He captured her lips with his, parting them, slipping his tongue into the sweet darkness of her mouth. She sank her fingers into his thick hair and returned the kiss, giving as much as she was receiving.

Richard ended the kiss to move to one of her breasts that was fuller from her pregnancy, more lush and womanly. Her hands fluttered over his back, savoring the feel of the taut muscles, the very strength and power of him.

They didn't think, not there in their stolen, private

place, they only felt, cherishing every sensual sensation, every heady aroma, every treasure newly found as lips and hands rediscovered what was theirs to have...one last glorious time.

It was theirs.

And it was ecstasy.

The flames of desire within them grew hotter, licking throughout them, burning.

"Bren," Richard said.

"Yes. Oh, yes, Richard."

He entered her slowly, holding back, being so very careful, until she was tossing her head restlessly on the pillow, wanting more, needing more, all of him. Brenda raised her hips and he surged within her, filling her, bringing a soft sigh of feminine pleasure whispering from her lips.

They moved as one in perfect rhythm. It wasn't a Strauss waltz, nor a Texas two-step, it was a dance they created just for themselves, together. They were caught in the swirl of the heat of desire, flung higher as the crescendo neared, the music theirs alone to hear.

It thrummed. Higher, hotter, faster. Beating in a wild tempo, carrying them up and away to finally burst into wondrous oblivion while each called the other's name.

They drifted, lingered, as the music became dreamy, soothing, quiet and serene.

Richard moved off Brenda, then gathered her into his arms, holding her close.

Then they each, so reverently, so tenderly, tucked the precious memories of what they had just shared in treasure chests in their hearts and minds.

Hearts quieted. Bodies cooled. Reality rose to the fore.

With an unspoken agreement, knowing it was how it had to be, Richard eased off the bed, pulled on his clothes and left.

And when the apartment door closed behind him with a click, Brenda wept for all that might have been, but would never be.

Ten

Days slid into weeks, then into months, with time passing so quickly that Brenda felt on occasion that the baby would be born before she could possibly be prepared for her arrival.

Those weepy, panicky moments usually descended upon her when she was extremely tired, and she would share her dismay with Richard, who would whip out the list they had made of what had to be done, show her how many things were already crossed off as completed and tell her that everything was under control.

Brenda would wipe away her tears with yet another of Richard's handkerchiefs, allow him to soothe her fears, then her sunny smile would return.

Brenda's parents telephoned from Greece the minute they read the letter. They were totally supportive, expressed excitement over being grandparents and offered to fly home immediately to be with Brenda through the remaining months of her pregnancy.

She assured them that it wasn't necessary. She felt fine, fat but fine, and was surrounded by the MacAllister family, all of whom were being wonderful to her.

In her letter she'd said that she had no plans to marry the father of her baby. During the telephone conversation, her folks did not ask, nor did Brenda volunteer, the name of that man.

Richard and Jack painted the second bedroom in Brenda's apartment the pale-yellow she selected, then nursery furniture from the MacAllister stash was put into place.

A baby shower was held in Brenda's honor, per MacAllister tradition, and Brenda arranged the precious, tiny clothes in the dresser drawers in the nursery. She then proceeded to take everything out again, just so she could see and touch each delicate item.

Richard enlisted Brenda's help in decorating the office he had rented for his new company, Mac-Allister Technical Services.

She dragged him from store to store to find the perfect furniture for the reception area, and also stated he had to have an impressive desk befitting the oh-so-important owner of a company.

Richard went to the northern part of California for a week to meet with various computer supply outlets in Silicone Valley, finally reaching an agreement with one that was able to provide the equipment that Richard anticipated needing.

He was also busy interviewing and hiring com-

puter troubleshooters to make up his crew. Brenda
investigated and compared group medical insurance
packages, finally presenting her choice to Richard as
being the best one for him to offer his employees.

Richard and Brenda attended a potluck Thanksgiving dinner at Jillian and Forrest's home. It was a
fun day with the noise level, Robert MacAllister declared, probably registering on the Richter scale.

The large house was overflowing with adults and
children, never-ending football games blared from
the television with a male audience of well-fed
MacAllisters hooting and hollering, and kids were
everywhere in every shape, size and temperament.

Except for a few knowing nods directed at Brenda
from Margaret MacAllister, no one behaved any differently toward Brenda, nor did they remark on the
fact that she and Richard had arrived at the festivities
together. After all, Brenda surmised, she and Richard
had attended many family events together in the past.

The days flew by.

The nights did not.

During the quiet hours in the darkness, Brenda
found herself, time and again, reliving the exquisitely
beautiful lovemaking she had shared with Richard.
She would be overcome with desire, then in the next
moment she would be consumed with a chilling
sense of loneliness as her hand swept over the empty
expanse of bed next to her.

In the light of the new day she would push the
images of the previous night from her mind, chalk
up the whole nonsense to her pregnant hormones and
go blissfully off to work at the travel agency.

During the first week in December, Brenda had an

appointment with Kara. After the examination Brenda eased herself into the chair opposite Kara's desk in her office and sighed.

"Kara, I have two months to go and I feel as though I'm going to explode any minute," Brenda said. "I'm huge. I can't even remember when I looked like I was smuggling a basketball." She rested her hands on her stomach. "This is the Goodyear blimp that got lost on its way to a football stadium."

"Mmm," Kara said as she wrote some data in Brenda's chart. She flipped the file closed, folded her hands on the top of it and frowned. "Your blood pressure is up again, Brenda. Are you certain that you're not sneaking some salt into your diet?"

"I promise I'm not," Brenda said, raising one hand. "Everything tastes so bland and...I didn't realize how much flavor salt added to food, until I couldn't have it anymore. Blak."

"Well, the holidays are coming, and that means all kinds of temptations as far as food goes," Kara said. "You are set on automatic 'no.' No salt...none. That means no baked goods. I also don't like the degree of swelling in your feet and ankles. You have got to slow down, quit doing so much, spend more time relaxing with your tootsies up."

Brenda's eyes widened. "Slow down? Now? I'm about to start my Christmas shopping."

"That's what mail-order catalogs are for, as well as shopping on the Internet, Brenda," Kara said, "I'm serious. You come home from work and stay put. There will be no grabbing a bite to eat and heading for the malls to Christmas shop for you. Are you listening to me?''

''Yes,'' Brenda said, nodding. ''Kara, you're not smiling, not even a little. Is something wrong? With me? With the baby?''

''I'm a little concerned,'' Kara said, leaning back in her chair. ''The baby has started to turn and drop a bit already and it's awfully early for that. I don't want you doing anything that will bring on early labor. I'm going to start scheduling you for weekly appointments so I can keep close tabs on you. You'll probably go full term to February first, but let's not take any chances.''

''You're frightening me, Kara,'' Brenda said, the color draining from her face.

''I'm sorry, but you have to hear this. If I don't like what I see at any point, I'm going to order complete bed rest. That isn't necessary yet, but don't be surprised if I tell you very soon that you can only work half days at the travel agency. I'd rather be overcautious, Brenda, than have that little one come earlier than is best for her.''

''Yes. Yes, of course, I understand,'' Brenda said.

''With Richard not traveling the way he used to,'' Kara said, ''he's right next door and should be able to help you. Right?''

''He's putting in very long hours at his new office,'' Brenda said. ''He's mapping out advertising campaigns, calling prospective customers, still interviewing candidates to work for him and—''

''Whoa,'' Kara said, raising one hand. ''Richard MacAllister is also going to be a father, and there are responsibilities that go along with that role.

Would you like me to talk to him, explain that he needs to run your errands for you, cook dinner?''

"No, no, I'll tell Richard what you said," Brenda said. "He wants and loves this baby every bit as much as I do, Kara. He'll come through for me—" she splayed one hand on her stomach "—for us, I know he will. After all, he's my—"

"Yes, I know," Kara said, shaking her head. "Richard is your best friend." She paused. "Do you know that the triplets asked Jillian and Forrest why they, the girls, hadn't been invited to the wedding for Aunt Brenda and Uncle Richard?"

"What wedding?" Brenda said, confused. "There wasn't any wedding."

"The girls were convinced there had been, and their feelings were hurt because they didn't get to attend. Jessica said that she was sure there was a wedding, because Aunt Brenda and Uncle Richard smile at each other with warm eyes just like her mommy and daddy do. The girls said all this after seeing you and Richard together on Thanksgiving."

"Oh," Brenda said, smoothing her maternity smock over her stomach. "Well, aren't kids just the cutest thing? 'Smile at each other with warm eyes.' Isn't that sweet? Of course, they misinterpreted what they were seeing, but that's understandable. The triplets are only six years old. What do they know about love, being *in* love and...stuff?"

"More to the point," Kara said, leaning forward, "what do *you* know about the subject?"

"Well, I admit that I'm no expert," Brenda said, lifting her chin, "but I certainly know the difference between loving someone as a best friend and being *in* love with the person who is your soul mate, your forever, your— Yes, I do, no doubt about it. Those two kinds of love aren't even in the same arena, the same stratosphere, the same… You get the drift.''

''Mmm,'' Kara said. ''You mentioned in the examining room that you were worried about Richard because he was working so hard getting this new company of his off the ground.''

''Oh, he is, Kara,'' Brenda said, nodding. ''He's putting in terribly long days, is forgetting to eat and…he has dark smudges under his eyes, and he looks exhausted more often than he should. He's happy, though, very excited about this new adventure of his, and that's worth a lot, but I do wish he was taking better care of himself.''

''And you're also positive that Richard will rally when you tell him that I've ordered you to slow down and take things easy,'' Kara said.

''I know he will, because he loves this baby,'' Brenda said, patting her stomach.

''Oh, for heaven's sake, Bren,'' Kara said, throwing up her hands, ''did it ever occur to you that Richard loves *you,* is *in* love with *you,* isn't just centered on the child you're carrying? And did it ever occur to you that *you* are *in* love with him, too, and you just haven't realized it?''

''That's just not how it is between me and Richard,'' Brenda said quietly. ''It just isn't. Kara, I'm not alone in my thinking. Richard and I have discussed this at length, and are in complete agreement on the subject. Being best friends is not enough to base a marriage on, and we're not in love with each other, so…'' She shrugged.

"Well, the MacAllister family vote is in to the contrary," Kara said, folding her arms over her chest, "and there's no doubt in anyone's mind that Richard is the baby's father. Oh, don't worry. No one is going to start getting on your case about it, but the family truly believes that you and Richard are in love with each other and are too…too…well, there's no other word for it…too *dumb* to see what's right in front of your noses."

"Well, that's rude," Brenda said indignantly. "Calling us dumb. That's not very nice at all. I'm not surprised, I guess, that everyone figured out that Richard is the baby's father even though no one has said anything about it, but you people just don't understand the concept of being best friends without being *in* love because none of you have ever been in the emotional place where Richard and I are."

"And a whole group of people," Kara said, sweeping one hand through the air, "an entire family who cares about you are wrong?"

"Right," Brenda said. "They're wrong. Right." She leveled herself to her feet. "I must go. I'm meeting Richard for lunch so I can report on how my appointment with you went, and I'm sure you have other patients to see. 'Bye, Kara."

"Make an appointment for next week, Bren," Kara said. "And no salt. And stay off your feet as much as possible and—"

"Yes, yes, I've got it all memorized," Brenda said, smiling. "Come on, baby girl," she said, patting her stomach. "We've got a lunch date with your daddy."

* * *

Richard sat at a small round table in a pool of sunshine on the terrace of the restaurant where he'd agreed to meet Brenda for lunch.

The December day was crisp, and his first inclination had been to request a table inside where it was warmer. He'd hesitated, then asked the hostess if there was a free space on the terrace in the sunshine, knowing that Brenda would enjoy the fresh air.

He'd smiled his approval at the location of the table, ordered a soda and settled in to wait for Brenda. He was early for their date, he knew, but the extra time might be just what he needed to improve his lousy mood.

He poked an ice cube in his glass with the straw, watched the cube dunk under the dark liquid, then pop back up to the surface. He repeated the process, frowning as the ice once again appeared.

Dumb ice cube, he thought. It would keep struggling to the top, time after time, even though it was melting, growing smaller and smaller. It wouldn't give up. Then it would finally cease to exist, would just disappear as though it had never been there. All that effort, all that work, would have been for nothing.

Richard took the straw from the glass, dropped it onto the table, then rotated his neck back and forth with the hope of relaxing the knotted muscles.

He felt like that ice cube, he thought dismally. He was knocking himself out, putting in long hours that were physically and mentally draining, in an attempt to get his fledgling business off the ground. He was struggling to get to the top, just like the ice in the glass.

But there was a constant knot in his stomach stemming from the feeling that there was something wrong, something missing, something off-kilter about his new endeavor that was keeping him from being excited, enthused, filled with anticipation about the challenge that lay ahead.

Richard sighed and wrapped his hands around the tall, cold glass, staring into the drink at the ice cube.

If he melted, just disappeared, would it matter?

Well, yeah, sure it would. He had a large, extended family who loved him. He was going to be a daddy to a precious baby girl in two months. He had Brenda, his best friend, who was an integral part of his life, and vice versa. He had hired people who were now counting on him for their livelihood and careers.

Richard's hold on the glass tightened.

And it wasn't enough.

It all fell just short of his lifelong hopes and dreams.

And there, he thought, was the source of his discontent, the cause of the fist in his gut that grew bigger and colder with every passing day.

He was reaching for the gold ring on the merry-go-round and missing it by inches, was so close, so close, but just couldn't quite get ahold of it and claim it as his.

Dandy, he thought, shaking his head in self-disgust. He'd gone from being a melting ice cube to a kid on a carnival ride who wanted to go for the gold.

But he wasn't a child. He was a man. He was Richard MacAllister, who wanted, with every breath in his body, to be head over heels in love, to have a partner in life, a soul mate, to share the good times and bad.

He wanted a home overflowing with love and laughter, and the sound of happy children at play.

He wanted a wife, who would snuggle close to him in their bed at night after they'd made sweet, beautiful love, sleep with her head nestled by his on the same pillow, then wake up next to him at dawn's light.

He wanted it all.

But it wasn't going to happen.

Richard drained the glass, then thunked it back onto the table.

So close, he thought. The pieces were all there, scattered, but if he attempted to put them together to reveal the blissful picture of the puzzle, they wouldn't fit. Close, but not quite. No matter how much he attempted to force them into place, they wouldn't go, because they were all just a shade off the mark.

Yes, he was going to be a father, and that thought was terrifying and exciting and wonderful. But he wouldn't be sleeping down the hall from his daughter, ready to leap to his feet if she cried in the night. Hell, no, he would be in the apartment next door…alone…oblivious to his baby girl's needs.

He wouldn't live in a big, sunny home. He was sentenced to existing in a set of rooms that had a solid wall separating him from his child and her mother.

Brenda. His best friend, his buddy, his pal, who had devoted time and energy to helping him get his new office in shape, was so thrilled about his new adventure that her eyes virtually sparkled whenever they discussed his plans.

Brenda. He loved her. But, as she was so quick to point out when the subject was addressed, he wasn't *in* love with her, nor was she *in* love with him.

Such a small word, *in,* two little letters that represented the difference between him embracing every hope and dream he'd had for the future and where his reality really lay…just short, so close but not quite, an ice cube struggling to the surface time and again and not really getting anywhere by doing so.

MacAllister, he thought, get a grip. Get over it. Get with the program. The cards were dealt, he knew what he had in his hand, what was his and what wasn't.

And somehow, for his sake, as well as for Brenda's and the baby's, he had to make this work, find something to hang on to in this jumbled situation, a measure of happiness that would be enough to sustain him through the years ahead. Somehow.

Richard glanced up and saw Brenda at the far side of the terrace, scanning the crowd. He stood and waved to her, saw the smile that lit up her face as she waved back, then watched as she began to weave her way through the tables to join him.

God, she was beautiful, Richard thought. She was woman personified, the very essence of femininity. She waddled when she walked, her protruding stomach announcing to the world that she carried a miracle within her. A baby. *His* baby. *Their* baby girl.

The sunlight on the terrace was pouring over her like a golden waterfall, making her dark hair glisten and her skin glow. One of her delicate hands was resting protectively on her stomach in an instinctive desire to shield their child from harm. She was wearing a pretty pink dress with tiny pleats across the bodice and a soft bow at the neck. So lovely.

And, oh, man, he was so glad to see her.

Richard hurried to meet Brenda, wanting, needing, to close the distance between them. He was vaguely aware that with each step he took the cold fist in his gut was replaced with a soothing warmth that was causing a genuine smile to cover his face.

"Hi," Brenda said, when Richard reached her. "I hope I didn't keep you waiting long. The traffic was awful. I guess the Christmas shopping madness has begun."

Richard placed one hand on Brenda's cheek and looked directly into her eyes.

"Brenda, I—" He cleared his throat as strange and foreign emotions assaulted him. "I just want to tell you that…that you're the most beautiful woman I've ever seen. You truly are, Bren. I know you think you're fat and clumsy and…but you're not. You're exquisite."

"Thank you, Richard," Brenda whispered. "Oh, yes, thank you more than I can say, because I feel like a blimp, a whale, a— I'm beautiful?"

Richard kissed her on the forehead.

"You're beautiful," he said, his voice gritty. "Come sit down. I found a table in the sunshine just for you, but if you're chilly, just say the word and we'll move inside for lunch."

"Oh, no, it's so nice out here," Brenda said as they walked to the table. Richard assisted her with her chair, then settled on his own opposite her. "The sun feels heavenly. You know me so well, Richard. You knew I'd prefer to eat outside if it was possible, and this table is perfect. It's as though the sun is shining just for us."

"Yep," he said. "I told it to."

"Oh, okay," she said, laughing.

"Want a serving of trivia, my sweet?" Richard said, folding his arms over his chest.

"Yes, yes, yes," she said. "We've been so busy it's been ages since we've shared any trivia. First, though, I want to say that you look very dashing in your suit and tie, sir. What was on your agenda that called for you to wear your all-grown-up clothes?"

Richard laughed. "My big-boy duds, huh? I had a meeting with a banker to apply for a line of credit so I can bring in the computers I need when I need them."

"And?"

Richard snapped his fingers. "Piece of cake. I signed the papers, and it's a done deal."

"Oh, Richard, that's wonderful," Brenda said, clasping her hands beneath her chin. "This is all so exciting. At the rate you're going *your* new baby, MacAllister Technical Services, will be born before *my* baby."

Richard frowned. "They're both *ours,* Bren. The new company, Baby Girl MacAllister—they're both *ours.* You know that, don't you?"

"Well, yes, all right, Richard," Brenda said, matching his frown. "I didn't mean to upset you or— Are you feeling okay? You look so tired, and I'm worried that you're trying to do too much."

"I'm fine," he said. "You're worried about *me?* We're concentrating on *you* and that bundle you're lugging around there."

"You're just as important as I am, Richard," Brenda said, "and just as important as Flash. We're all in this together, you know."

Together, Richard thought. No, not quite. Close, very close, but not quite.

"Right," he said. "Back to the trivia. Madam, I want you to know that the first toilet ever seen on television was on *Leave It to Beaver.*"

"No kidding?" the waitress said, appearing at their table. "I loved that show when I was a kid. I used to drive my mom nuts because I kept telling her she should wear dresses and pearls to cook dinner like Beaver's mother. First toilet on the tube, huh? Amazing. So! What can I bring you folks for lunch? Oops. You don't even have menus. I'll be right back."

The woman hurried away, and Brenda drew a deep breath and let it out slowly.

"I have to order something that is totally salt free," she said quietly. "Kara is a bit concerned about my blood pressure and the swelling in my feet and—

"Oh, darn it, Richard, I can't even go Christmas shopping because Kara said I have to stay off my feet and order gifts from catalogs, and she might insist that I cut back on my hours at the travel agency, but that isn't for certain yet, and…when I come home from work I'm not to cook, or clean, or do the laundry. I'm just supposed to sit there like a lump with my feet up and...I was doing all right with all of this until I saw you, but now I'm falling apart and...oh, God, Richard, I'm so frightened that something is going to happen to our baby.''

A chill swept through Richard with such force he had to take a sharp breath against the sudden pain. His hands shot out and gripped Brenda's, holding them tightly on the top of the table as he leaned toward her.

"Listen to me," he said, his heart racing. "Everything is going to be fine. We'll follow Kara's orders to the letter, do everything she says. It just rips me up to see you so upset, so scared, Bren. You're not alone. I'm here, right here with you, and I always will be. We'll get through this, you'll see. We'll do it...together.''

"Yes.'' Brenda produced a rather wobbly smile. "Yes...together. Everything will be all right...as long as we're together.''

Eleven

Richard opened Brenda's apartment door, hesitated, then closed the door again. He strode across the room to the sofa, where Brenda was sitting with her feet propped up on the coffee table.

"Are you positive that you won't let me call someone from the family to come stay with you while I'm gone?" he said, frowning.

Brenda smiled up at him. "Richard, I'll be perfectly fine here alone. I'm following Kara's orders to the letter. Right? I've only been working half days for the past week. Right? Tomorrow is Christmas Eve and the agency is closed, so I'll be sitting here vegging. Right? And you'll be back tomorrow afternoon. Right?"

"Right," he said, dragging one hand through his

hair. "I wish your folks were arriving from Greece today instead of tomorrow night."

"They couldn't get plane reservations for any earlier. They let it go too late and—" Brenda laughed. "They should be organized like their daughter.

"Richard, shoo. You're going to miss your plane and have to take a different one. Then you'll be late arriving in San Francisco, and you'll miss your meeting with the hotshot computer ace you want to entice to come work for you. He's only going to be in the airport for a few hours between flights before he wings his way home for Christmas."

"Yeah, well, it's because of the holidays that I couldn't get another flight back here until tomorrow afternoon." Richard shook his head. "No, I don't need that guy all that much. I'm not going. Nope. No way."

"Oh, good grief," Brenda said, rolling her eyes heavenward. "I promise that I'll hardly move while you're gone. You bought me my very own video of *Casablanca* and enough magazines and books to last me six months. The refrigerator and cupboards are full and…Richard, your concern is so dear and I really appreciate it, but I'm going to be just fine. Now…go."

"Well…"

"I'm going to sit right here and look at our beautiful Christmas tree," Brenda went on. "Our daughter is going to adore hearing the story about how you were decorating the tree, with me giving directions from my perch here on the sofa, and when you put the angel on the top, you looked at me and said,

'Let's name our baby Angela, because she's going to be our little angel.' Ohhh, that is so-o-o sweet.''

Richard laughed. ''And you get weepy every time you think about it. Okay, Bren, I'll go on this junket. But, you have my cell phone number, the hotel number and my pager number.'' He leaned over and kissed Brenda on the forehead, then patted her stomach. ''Bye, Angela Jane. Be a good girl for your mommy.''

''My mother is going to be so thrilled when we tell her we're naming the baby Jane, after her.''

''I'm surprised she was *thrilled* when you finally told her that I'm the baby's father. She actually said that she and your father have always liked me? Think I'll be a great daddy?''

''Yep,'' Brenda said, nodding. ''Goodbye, Richard.''

Richard hunkered down next to the sofa and looked directly into Brenda's eyes.

''I'll be thinking about you and Angela,'' he said. ''Take care of yourself, Bren.''

''I will,'' she said softly. ''Don't worry.''

A long moment passed, then Richard sighed and stood again.

''I'm gone,'' he said. ''I'll call you tonight from the hotel.''

''Bye.''

When Richard left the apartment and closed the door behind him, a heavy silence fell over the room, and Brenda frowned. She splayed her hands on her stomach.

''Well, here we are, Angela Jane. Want to watch

Casablanca? Angela Jane what…? Your daddy and I still haven't settled on how to handle your last name. Angela Jane Henderson-MacAllister? That's an awfully big title for a little girl. Oh, well, there's still plenty of time left to get that figured out.''

Brenda shifted her gaze to the Christmas tree.

If things were different, she thought, they would all be MacAllisters. Brenda, Richard and Angela MacAllister. A family. A mother, father and baby. A wife, husband and daughter. A—no, there was no sense dwelling on what wasn't going to be.

"Just don't go there, Brenda," she said, then picked up one of the magazines from the stack next to her. "Oh, mercy, look at all that yummy holiday food. Forget it. I'm going to watch my movie."

Later that night, Brenda smiled as she replaced the telephone receiver after a long conversation with Richard. She snapped off the light on the nightstand next to the bed and wiggled until she was in a comfortable position.

Richard had sounded so pleased with himself, she thought, staring up into the darkness. The man he'd met with was going to talk to his wife about moving to Ventura, a plan that the guy thought would be well received since his family had had enough of Minnesota winters.

She'd humored Richard by telling him everything she'd done since he'd left and detailed every morsel of salt-free food she'd placed in her mouth.

His San Francisco trivia had been terrific. There

were 336 dimples on a regulation golf ball. Fascinating. Richard sure was a pro at trivia.

Brenda yawned, then her lashes drifted down as she floated off to sleep.

Three hours later Brenda opened her eyes and wondered foggily why she was awake. In the next moment she gasped as a sharp pain sliced low and deep through her body.

As the pain eased, she took a steadying breath and willed her racing heart to slow its wild tempo.

Whatever that had been, she thought, it was over. She would just blank her mind and go back to sleep and—

"Oh!" she said, as another pain rocketed through her.

She gripped the blankets tightly until the agony stopped, then leveled herself up to the side of the bed. As she got to her feet, a rush of liquid soaked her nightgown and the carpet where she was standing.

"Oh, God, no," she said, her voice trembling. "My water broke." She splayed her hands on her stomach. "Angela, no, not yet, baby. It's too soon. You can't come yet. Richard. Oh, God, Richard, I need you. Please, Richard?"

Calm down, Brenda, she told herself, as she turned on the light.

She sat down on the bed, took an address book from the nightstand drawer, then picked up the receiver to the telephone with a shaking hand. She opened the book, pressed the numbers written on the page, made a mistake that caused her to whimper, then tried again. A telephone rang on the other end of the line.

"Dr. MacAllister."

"Kara?" Brenda said. "It's Brenda. Oh, Kara, my water broke, and I'm having sharp pains, and it's too early for Angela to be born and—"

"Easy, easy," Kara said. "Have Richard bring you to the hospital right away. I'll meet you there."

"Richard isn't here," Brenda said, her eyes filling with tears. "He had to fly to San Francisco and… He's not here, Kara."

"Darn it," Kara said. "Okay. Brenda, don't panic, all right? I'm going to have an ambulance come for you. That's the safest way to do this. Unlock the door so the paramedics can get in. Don't bother getting fully dressed, just put on a fresh nightgown. Are you with me here?"

"Unlock the door. Fresh nightgown," Brenda said, nodding. "But what about the baby? She isn't supposed to be born yet, Kara."

"Angela obviously doesn't want to miss the Christmas festivities," Kara said. "She's definitely about to greet the world. I'll have the preemie team standing by, Bren. Angela will get the very best care there is, I promise. Now, hang up the phone so we can get this show on the road."

"I…yes…'bye."

Brenda replaced the receiver, then wrapped her arms around her stomach and bent over as another pain assaulted her. When the pain subsided, she picked up a piece of paper from the nightstand. A few moments later she burst into tears when Richard answered the ringing on the line with a mumbled "What!"

"Richard? Oh, God, Richard, the baby is coming," she said, a sob catching in her throat. "Now. My water broke and Kara is sending an ambulance, and I'm so scared because Angela is too early. It's not time yet, Richard, and she'll be so small and—"

"Brenda, are you sure that— Ah, damn, of course, you are. Your water broke. I'm on my way... somehow. I'll get on a plane if I have to hijack one. Oh, God, Bren, I'm so sorry I'm not there with you. I'm so, so sorry, Bren, and I love you so much, and I'll be there just as quickly as I can, and Angela will be fine...you'll see. I love you, Brenda, with all my heart, mind and soul."

"I love you, too, Richard," Brenda said, crying openly. "I love you so very much. I need you here with me, because you're my soul mate and this is our baby and...hurry, Richard. Please."

"Yes," he said, then slammed down the receiver.

"Your daddy is coming home," Brenda said, sobbing as she patted her stomach. "He's on his way to help us, Angela. Unlock the door. Put on a clean nightie. I can do that. And Richard will be here...soon."

Four hours later Richard dashed out of the elevator on the maternity floor of Mercy Hospital and ran down the corridor to the nurses' station. His hair was tousled, and his shirttail was hanging out beneath his short winter jacket. He skidded to a halt at the counter and leaned forward.

"I'm Brenda," he said breathlessly. "No, that's not right. I'm Richard. Richard MacAllister, and I'm here. I made it. Chartered a plane and— Where's Brenda? I have to go to her, be with her, let her know I'm here for her and— Where did you put Brenda?"

The nurse behind the counter smiled. "Get a grip, Dad, or we'll end up with you in a hospital bed, too." She glanced at a piece of paper on her desk. "I don't have a Brenda MacAllister on this floor."

"No, no," Richard said, "she's Brenda Henderson. My sister is her doctor…Kara MacAllister."

"Ah," the nurse said, nodding. "Yes, Brenda Henderson. Here she is." She looked at Richard again. "If you'll go into the waiting room right across the hall, there, I'll inform Dr. MacAllister that you're here."

"But…" Richard drummed his fingers on the countertop. "Okay, okay, but hurry, all right? Please?"

"Yes, I'll hurry." The nurse pointed to the waiting room. "Go."

Richard spun around and strode across the hallway, muttering under his breath as he went. He entered the room and stopped so suddenly he staggered slightly.

They were all there. The MacAllisters. A representative from each of the families, plus his parents and his aunt Margaret and uncle Robert.

Richard's heart thudded in his chest and he shook

his head, unable to speak for a moment. His mother came to him and gave him a hug.

"You made it, dear," she said. "That's wonderful. It will mean so much to Brenda."

"Do you know anything?" Richard said. "What's going on? How's Brenda? Ah, man, *where* is Brenda? Damn it, I should never have left her alone. She's so scared, so— And the baby— It's too soon for Angela to be born, Mom. She'll be so small and—"

"Whoa, brother," Jack said, crossing the room. "Take it easy, Richard. You won't do Brenda any good if you're falling apart. Kara was here for a moment and said she has the preemie team standing by to tend to the baby the minute she's born. Brenda's labor was moving right along with no complications."

"But..." Richard said.

"Richard MacAllister?" a nurse said from the doorway.

"Me!" he yelled, turning in the direction of the voice.

The nurse held up a green scrub top that had ties along the back. "There's no time for you to change into the full garb. Stick your arms in this and follow me into the delivery room. You're about two contractions away from becoming a father."

"Ohmigod," Richard whispered.

"Move," Jack said, whopping his brother on the back.

It was a blur. Richard was vaguely aware of putting on the green top, rushing after the nurse, then

entering a brightly lit room that seemed to be overflowing with people in white uniforms. Someone
pressed on his shoulders, he sat down on a stool, then
blinked as he found himself staring at Brenda.

"Bren?" he said tentatively.

Brenda turned her head. "Oh, Richard. Oh, Richard, you're here." She raised one hand, and he
grasped it in both of his. "I'm so glad to see you.
Don't leave me, Richard, please."

"Never," he said, tightening his hold on her hand.

"Welcome to the party, big brother," Kara said
from the other end of the delivery table. "You cut it
close, but you made it."

"Ohhh," Brenda moaned, attempting to sit up.

Richard's eyes widened. "Bren? What? What?"

"Support her back, Richard," Kara said. "Okay,
Brenda, this is it. Push for me now, sweetie. That's
it. A little more. Here…she…comes. Yes!"

With a swoop, Kara laid the wailing baby on
Brenda's stomach.

"Oh, Richard," Brenda said, tears streaming down
her face as she touched one of the baby's tiny hands,
"look at her. She's here. Our Angela. Our miracle."

"Yeah," Richard said, awe ringing in his voice as
he made no attempt to hide the tears shimmering in
his own eyes. "Our daughter."

A group of people moved forward, and the baby
was whisked quickly away. Richard eased Brenda
back to lie down, then wiped her tears away with his
thumbs.

"She's so tiny," Brenda said, her voice trembling.

"She came too soon, Richard, and—" Tears choked off her words.

"Five pounds, one ounce," someone called from across the room.

"Fantastic," Kara said, then stood and walked to the head of the table. "You did beautifully, Brenda."

"Angela?" Brenda said.

"She's a good weight," Kara said. "Excellent. Our concern is her lungs because she came so early. She's being checked over now, head to toe, by the experts. From the sound of her none-too-quiet arrival, I'd say her lungs are fine, but we have to be certain. We'll have a complete report in a little while."

"How long is a little while?" Richard said.

"Soon," Kara said, smiling. "Richard, go tell the family the news while we finish up here, then you can see Brenda in her room in a bit."

"How long is a bit?" Richard said.

"Get out of here," Kara said, laughing. "Give Brenda a kiss, thank her for your lovely daughter, then go."

"Oh." Richard gave Brenda a quick kiss on the lips. "Thank you for our lovely daughter, then go." He shook his head slightly. "I don't feel very well."

"Mick," Kara called, "we've got a daddy turning out the lights over here."

A big, burly man ran across the room and caught Richard just as he toppled backward off the stool.

"Richard?" Brenda said, raising up on one elbow.

Mick hoisted Richard over his shoulder in a fireman's carry and left the delivery room.

"Richard!" Brenda yelled.

Kara laughed and patted Brenda on the shoulder, urging her to lie flat again. "He'll be fine, Bren. His biggest problem will be that he'll never live this down. The MacAllister clan is going to have a field day with this one."

"Poor Richard," Brenda said. "Kara, do you really think Angela is all right?"

"We'll know soon. Just relax."

As Kara returned to the other end of the table, tears filled Brenda's eyes again.

"But how long is soon?" she whispered.

After Richard was deposited in the waiting room by Mick, and the nurse on duty told the group to hold down the noise created by their hooting and hollering over Richard's performance, the family grew serious, waiting for word on the baby.

Kara finally appeared and motioned to a pale Richard to follow her as she told the family she'd be right back to bring them up to date.

In Brenda's room, where she was propped up against the pillows on the bed, Kara told the new parents that Angela Jane was absolutely fine. She was going to be in an incubator for the next twenty-four hours just as a safety precaution. Kara explained that newborns usually lose weight at first, and Angela could go home once she was a steady five pounds.

"Any questions?" she said to Brenda and Richard.

"No," Brenda said. "Thank you so much, Kara."

"I'll go tell the family," Kara said, "give them a peek at Angela, then send everyone home. Richard, you have ten minutes, then Brenda is going to get some well-deserved rest.''

After Kara left, a silence fell over the room that stretched from one minute into an uncomfortable two, then three.

Dear heaven, Brenda thought frantically, she'd told Richard that she loved him, and he had said that he loved her and...not best-friend love, but *in* love love. That was what they'd declared for each other on the telephone.

They'd both been very upset and scared and...people said things under stressful circumstances that they really didn't mean and shouldn't be held accountable for and—

Oh, God, who was she kidding?

She *did* love Richard MacAllister. She was *in* love with him. When it had actually happened, she didn't know. All she was certain of was that she loved Richard with all her heart. Her best friend was her soul mate, just as the MacAllisters had tried to explain.

But Richard mustn't know how she felt. It would ruin everything, put such a strain on their friendship, their relationship, as they raised Angela. She would keep her secret wrapped tightly in her heart.

''Bren,'' Richard said, breaking the heavy silence and causing Brenda to jerk at the sudden sound of his voice. ''We need to talk about what we said to each other on the phone when you called to tell me that Angela was on the way.''

''Oh, that,'' Brenda said, waving one hand breezily in the air. ''Wasn't that silly? There's probably some trivia recorded somewhere about how many people blither nonsense when they're stressed to the max. Don't give it another thought, Richard. I certainly won't.

"Well, it's been quite a night, and I'm exhausted. I'm so grateful that Angela is going to be all right. I can hardly wait to hold her and—" tears filled Brenda's eyes "—I think...you'd better go."

Brenda met Richard's gaze for the first time since Kara had left the room and frowned when she saw what appeared to be a flicker of...what? What was that? Sadness...pain...in his dark, expressive MacAllister eyes? No, he was just tired after all that had transpired tonight.

"Well," Richard said, then drew a deep breath and let it out slowly. "Yes. You want me to go, so...I'll shove off. We got ourselves quite a Christmas present, didn't we? Angela Jane... We never did figure out what we were going to do about her last name. I guess...I guess you'd really like it to be Henderson, huh?" He cleared his throat. "Good night, Brenda."

Richard hurried from the room, and two tears spilled onto Brenda's cheeks.

"I want Angela's name to be MacAllister," she said, sniffling, "and I want *my* name to be MacAllister. I want us *all* to be MacAllisters, a family. I love you with in-love kind of love, Richard, but you only love me with best-friend love and— Aaakk!"

Brenda shrieked as Richard came barreling back into the room.

"Damn it, Brenda," Richard said, "I can't carry this around inside me because I'll explode."

"What are you talking about?" she said, staring at him with wide eyes.

"I meant every word I said to you on the telephone," he said, volume on high. "I didn't know I meant it when I said it, I just said it, then I had that awful ten-year-long flight in that skinny little plane to get here, and I thought about it, really thought about it, and...

"Ah, Bren, I do love you so damn much. You're my best friend in the whole world, and you're also my soul mate, my other half, the mother of my child and the woman I want to spend the rest of my life with.

"I'm *in* love with you, Bren, and I know that gums up the works, and I pray this won't ruin our friendship, our raising Angela together, but— I apologize for not sticking to our program, but...good night, Brenda."

Richard got as far as grabbing the handle on the door.

"I love you, too, Richard MacAllister," Brenda said, a sob catching in her throat. "I meant what I said on the phone. You're my best friend, will always be my best friend, but you're also the man I love with every breath in my body. I'm *in* love with you, Richard MacAllister."

Richard turned around slowly and raised one finger in the air.

"Say that again," he said, narrowing his eyes.

"I'm in love with you, Richard."

"Ah, Bren. Does this mean you'll marry me? Be my wife? Does it?"

"Yes, yes, yes."

Richard closed the distance between them, cradled Brenda's face in his hands and kissed her.

It was a kiss of tenderness, of heartfelt devotion, of commitment, and the blending so perfectly together of the essence of friendship and the love between a man and a woman that would withstand the rigors of time.

It was a kiss of forever.

"Oops, excuse me," Kara said, coming into the room. "I came to boot you out of here, Richard, because I had a feeling you wouldn't leave in ten minutes. I also brought you two a picture of Angela, since she can't come visit you right now." She paused. "Could you come up for air and take this picture?"

Richard broke the kiss and straightened, smiling at Kara as he accepted the picture.

"Look, Bren," he said. "There she is. Tiny but perfect. Our daughter."

"She's so beautiful," Brenda said.

"Oh, one last thing," Kara said. "They asked me to find out the last name you want printed on Angela Jane's birth certificate."

"MacAllister," Brenda and Richard said in unison.

"Okay," Kara said, laughing. "That's clear enough."

"And you're invited to the wedding, little sister," Richard said.

"I knew I would be," Kara said. "I've already bought a new dress. It's about time you two came to your senses. Okay, Richard, I'm going to stand outside the door and wait for you. You have exactly one minute left to be with Brenda."

Kara made her exit, then Richard smiled warmly at Brenda.

"Kara is wrong," he said. "We have a lifetime left to be together, Bren."

"Yes," Brenda said, love shining in her eyes. "We have our very own forever, Richard...together."

*   *   *   *   *

Joan Elliott Pickart's
THE BABY BET

continues in
Silhouette Special Edition
in early 2001.

Don't miss
HER LITTLE SECRET,

a must-read romance
featuring confirmed bachelor
Sheriff Cable Montana!

Desire celebrates Silhouette's 20th anniversary in grand style!

Don't miss:

• *The Dakota Man* by Joan Hohl
Another unforgettable MAN OF THE MONTH
On sale October 2000

• *Marriage Prey* by Annette Broadrick
Her special anniversary title!
On sale November 2000

• *Slow Fever* by Cait London
Part of her new miniseries FREEDOM VALLEY
On sale December 2000

Plus:

FORTUNE'S CHILDREN: THE GROOMS
On sale August through December 2000
Exciting new titles from Leanne Banks, Kathryn Jensen,
Shawna Delacorte, Caroline Cross and Peggy Moreland

Every woman wants to be loved…
BODY & SOUL
Desire's highly sensuous new promotion features stories
from Jennifer Greene, Anne Marie Winston
and Dixie Browning!

Available at your favorite retail outlet.

Visit Silhouette at www.eHarlequin.com

PS20SD

#1 *New York Times* bestselling author

NORA ROBERTS

introduces the loyal and loving, tempestuous and
tantalizing Stanislaski family.

Coming in November 2000:

The Stanislaski Brothers
Mikhail and Alex

Their immigrant roots and warm, supportive home had
made Mikhail and Alex Stanislaski both strong and
passionate. And their charm makes them irresistible....

In February 2001, watch for
THE STANISLASKI SISTERS: Natasha and Rachel

And a brand-new Stanislaski story from Silhouette Special Edition,
CONSIDERING KATE

Available at your favorite retail outlet.

Where love comes alive™

If you enjoyed what you just read,
then we've got an offer you can't resist!

Take 2 bestselling love stories FREE!

Plus get a FREE surprise gift!

You're not going to believe this offer!

In October and November 2000, buy any two Harlequin or Silhouette books and save $10.00 off future purchases, or buy any three and save $20.00 off future purchases!

Just fill out this form and attach 2 proofs of purchase (cash register receipts) from October and November 2000 books and Harlequin will send you a coupon booklet worth a total savings of $10.00 off future purchases of Harlequin and Silhouette books in 2001. Send us 3 proofs of purchase and we will send you a coupon booklet worth a total savings of $20.00 off future purchases.

Saving money has never been this easy.

I accept your offer! Please send me a coupon booklet:

Name: _____

Address: _____ City: _____

State/Prov.: _____ Zip/Postal Code: _____

Optional Survey!

In a typical month, how many Harlequin or Silhouette books would you buy <u>new</u> at retail stores?

☐ Less than 1   ☐ 1   ☐ 2   ☐ 3 to 4   ☐ 5+

Which of the following statements best describes how you <u>buy</u> Harlequin or Silhouette books? Choose one answer only that <u>best</u> describes you.

☐ I am a regular buyer and reader
☐ I am a regular reader but buy only occasionally
☐ I only buy and read for specific times of the year, e.g. vacations
☐ I subscribe through Reader Service but also buy at retail stores
☐ I mainly borrow and buy only occasionally
☐ I am an occasional buyer and reader

Which of the following statements best describes how you <u>choose</u> the Harlequin and Silhouette series books you buy <u>new</u> at retail stores? By "series," we mean books within a particular line, such as *Harlequin PRESENTS* or *Silhouette SPECIAL EDITION.* Choose one answer only that <u>best</u> describes you.

☐ I only buy books from my favorite series
☐ I generally buy books from my favorite series but also buy books from other series on occasion
☐ I buy some books from my favorite series but also buy from many other series regularly
☐ I buy all types of books depending on my mood and what I find interesting and have no favorite series

Please send this form, along with your cash register receipts as proofs of purchase, to:
In the U.S.: Harlequin Books, P.O. Box 9057, Buffalo, NY 14269
In Canada: Harlequin Books, P.O. Box 622, Fort Erie, Ontario L2A 5X3

(Allow 4-6 weeks for delivery) Offer expires December 31, 2000.   PHQ4002

COMING NEXT MONTH

#1327 MARRIAGE PREY—Annette Broadrick
Until she found herself stranded on an isolated island with irresistibly handsome police detective Steve Antonelli, red-hot passion had just been one of overprotected Robin McAlister's fantasies. Could her sizzling romance with an experienced man like Steve develop into a lasting love?

#1328 HER PERFECT MAN—Mary Lynn Baxter
Man of the Month
Strong-willed minister Bryce Burnette and flamboyant Katherine Mays couldn't have been more different. Only the fierce desire and tender love this red-haired beauty was stirring up inside Bryce would be able to dissolve the barriers that separated them.

#1329 A COWBOY'S GIFT—Anne McAllister
Code of the West
Rodeo cowboy Gus Holt had to do a whole lot more than turn on his legendary charm if he wanted to win back the heart of schoolteacher Mary McLean. He'd have to prove—in a very special way—that this time he was offering her a lifetime of love.

#1330 HUSBAND—OR ENEMY?—Caroline Cross
Fortune's Children: The Grooms
Angelica Dodd was powerfully drawn to—and pregnant by—charismatic bad boy Riley Fortune. But trusting him was another matter. Could Riley open his hardened heart and show her that they shared more than a marriage of convenience?

#1331 THE VIRGIN AND THE VENGEFUL GROOM—Dixie Browning
The Passionate Powers/Body & Soul
Even his tough training as a navy SEAL hadn't given Curt Powers the wherewithal to resist a virginal beauty like Lily O'Malley. He longed to take Lily—to make her his woman. But much to this confirmed bachelor's surprise, he also wanted to make her his *wife*.

#1332 NIGHT WIND'S WOMAN—Sheri WhiteFeather
The moment pregnant Kelly Baxter showed up at his door, Shane Night Wind knew his life was forever changed. How could he walk away from this woman in need? How could he protect his heart when Kelly and her baby could be his only salvation?